CONSIDER
THE LILLY

Other books by Sandra Carey Cody:

Put Out the Light

CONSIDER
THE LILLY

•

Sandra Carey Cody

AVALON BOOKS
NEW YORK

Published by Thomas Bouregy & Co., Inc.
160 Madison Avenue, New York, NY 10016

Library of Congress Cataloging-in-Publication Data

Cody, Sandra Carey.
    Consider the Lilly / Sandra Carey Cody.
        p. cm.
    ISBN 978-0-8034-9879-2 (acid-free paper)
    I. Title.

PS3603.O296C66   2008
813'.6—dc22   2007024172

PRINTED IN THE UNITED STATES OF AMERICA
ON ACID-FREE PAPER
BY HADDON CRAFTSMEN, BLOOMSBURG, PENNSYLVANIA

To Pete, my husband and my best friend.

Writing can be a lonely process, impossible to complete without the encouragement of trusted friends and readers. To my Sisters in Crime and Guppy critique partners, Debra Purdy Kong and Sheila Gallant-Halloran, thanks for your help. I know *Lilly* is a better book because of your advice. And to all my fellow mystery lovers at the Doylestown Library's Tuesday Night Group—Judy King, Sue Lyon, Laquita Wooddell, Mary Ellen Cannon, Sue Young, Nancy Mills, Karalee Ameel, Roberta Gledhill, Linda Seifried, Elaine Badcho—you are the best, most encouraging friends anyone could hope for. Thank you for believing in me and supporting me.

Chapter One

"Our stuff's gonna be cold."

"Lilly'll keep it warm for us."

"We're starving."

"You're not starving. You're bored."

"You can say that again." Tommy put in his two cents. Up to now he'd let Andy do the whining for both of them.

Jennie fed the last page of the report into the copier before she turned to her sons: nine-year-old Tommy and seven-year-old Andy. "Just a couple more minutes. Then we'll—"

Running footsteps thudded in the corridor. A white-coated figure darted past. Jennie sent up a prayer that Riverview's elderly residents were all okay. She had to know. A glance at the machine told her the report was copied.

"Tell you what, guys. Help me gather my stuff and we're outta here."

She stopped at the reception desk. "Woody passed the conference room in a rush. Everybody okay?"

"Everybody here's fine. Something's going on at Lilly's though."

Flashes of red, then blue, assaulted Jennie's senses when she opened the door. She squinted against the dizzying succession of color and tried to get an unobstructed view of the restaurant across the alley. She looked at the kids. "You guys wait inside."

Maybe they didn't hear. She knew that's what they'd say. At any rate, both boys ran ahead, down the ramp leading to the parking lot.

Jennie caught up and grabbed them before they could cross the alley. "Hey, I said, wait."

Andy, mesmerized by the swirling lights, didn't comment.

Tommy tried to wiggle free.

She kept a firm hand on each boy's shoulder and studied the commotion.

Emergency personnel were shoving a gurney into an ambulance. A uniformed cop stood between the ambulance, and a row of cars snugged against the back of the restaurant. Across the lot, a Memphis police car blocked the exit. Another officer stood by the vehicle. Dozens of people milled about, alternately watching the activity around the ambulance and casting furtive glances toward the police. She looked toward the ambulance. Was Lilly on that gurney? One of her kids? *I have to find out.*

She grabbed the kids' hands and approached the entrance to the parking lot.

The policeman stepped forward, but didn't speak. He stood, arms akimbo, shaking his head.

Jennie tried to explain. "That's my friend's restaurant. I need to know if she's okay."

"Sorry." He was a squat, burly man, shorter than Jennie's five foot seven inches, but somehow managed to convey the feeling he was looking down on her small family.

Tommy piped up, "What happened?"

"Nothing that concerns you." The cop's manner alarmed Jennie more than the emergency vehicles.

A van with a TV station's familiar blue and yellow logo rolled up. A large man with an elaborate camcorder hopped out, followed by a petite woman. Jennie recognized reporter Jill Newton.

Apparently the cop did, too. The would-be Napolean set his hat straight and tucked in his shirt before he sauntered toward the new arrivals.

Jennie took advantage of the distraction to edge closer.

The crowd parted and another gurney rolled out. A substantial female figure kept pace with the emergency workers who were maneuvering the gurney.

There's Lilly. Jennie expelled a breath she hadn't known she was holding. *At least it's not her in the ambulance.* She tried to read the situation by watching Lilly. She couldn't make out words, but her friend's posture and the movement of her hands said plenty. *This is serious. One of the girls?* Jennie sent up a silent prayer, *Please no,* and gripped her sons' hands tighter.

The thought of Lilly's daughters prompted Jennie to look toward the living quarters above the restaurant. A wide porch ran along the building's second story. Flood-lights, directed into the parking lot, left the porch in shadow. Something in the dim space behind the illumi-nated area caught her eye. A slender outline passed in front of one of the windows.

Jasmine? Probably. What's she up to?

Jennie used her hand to block the glare of the over-heard lights and watched the silhouette glide forward, peer over the railing, move back, hesitate, then inch along, keeping flat against the wall. At the porch's edge, the apparition climbed over the railing and disappeared.

Jennie looked toward the sturdy wooden arbor cover-ing the brick sidewalk that led from the parking lot to the main entrance in front. Her view was blocked, but she could guess what was happening. *Jasmine's sneak-ing out. Should I tell Lilly?* Jennie hated to do anything to fuel the already fiery relationship between mother and daughter. *On the other hand—if it were my sixteen-year-old . . .*

A stick-thin figure broke through the crowd, dashed to the ambulance, and started to climb in the back. A policeman ran after her, grabbed an arm, and hoisted her out. She screeched an epithet and tried to twist away but was no match for the much larger man. Long pale hair tinted an eerie red, then blue by the pulsing lights, hid her face, but her cries hung in the air, a pierc-ing banshee wail.

The reporter, followed by the rotund man and his camcorder, pushed through the crowd and held a micro-phone near the screaming woman.

Tommy's voice penetrated the din. "There's Woody. He'll know what's going on."

Jennie looked to where Tommy was pointing. At the center of the activity was Dr. Woodrow Samson. His presence and the memory of him running through Riverview's hall sent prickles of fear down her spine. She tried to piece together what must have happened. Ambulances are here, so they called nine-one-one. Why'd they need Woody? There was no good answer to that. Maybe they were scared, wanted a familiar face. Why? Another question with no good answer.

Woody closed the ambulance doors and stepped back. The vehicle pulled away, its siren wailing. He said something to one of the policemen, then turned.

The boys ran toward him, dragging their mother along.

"What happened?" Tommy asked.

"Some people got sick."

"One of Lilly's girls?" Jennie asked.

"No."

"Who?"

"Nobody you know." His curt tone surprised her. Woody was a good friend and usually took time to explain things to the kids. Tonight he dodged around them and hurried across the alley into Riverview.

Jennie looked back to the scene in the parking lot. The crowd was now clustered in groups. One woman stood alone a short distance from the others.

Jennie concentrated on her. She looked familiar.

The woman—tall, slender, dignified—did not join in the jostling and whispering. She stood apart, with her face directed not to the activity around the ambulance but outward, as though searching for someone in the crowd. Her gaze seemed to rest when it found Jennie, then flitted quickly away.

Odd. Where have I seen her? Unable to jog her memory, Jennie decided it was time to get her sons back to the safety of Riverview. "Come on, guys. It's freezing out here." That was true, or almost true. The temperature was slightly above freezing, but there was a damp chill to the air that penetrated the bones. It was only 6:30, but already dark on this Thursday in February.

The boys protested in unison. "I'm not cold."

"Well, I am," Jennie said. "Anyway, there's nothing more to see." She herded them across the alley, opened the door, and guided them through ahead of her. "How about a treat?"

"Like what?" Andy asked.

"Let's see what they have. Go get my purse. It's in the bottom drawer on the left side of my desk. I'll meet you at the vending machines."

No argument this time.

"Don't run!" she called after them, watching long enough to see that their pace wouldn't endanger any of Riverview's population.

Riverview Manor was a retirement community/nursing home that hugged the northern edge of Memphis, and Jennie was its activities director. As such, one of her responsibilities was to keep records of each resident's social interaction. This evening she'd come in to make copies of reports she would be presenting at a meeting the following morning.

When the kids disappeared around a corner, she turned for one last look through the small square of glass in the heavy door. The ambulance was gone, but the squad car still prevented a quick exit from the parking lot. Two policemen stood next to the vehicle. A third figure stood before them, arms waving, obviously distraught.

Jennie ignored the conflict and scanned the crowd, searching for Lilly Wainwright, co-owner and manager of the restaurant, and, much more important, a dear friend. She spotted Ward Norris, Lilly's self-appointed protector, but not Lilly. Maybe she went back inside.

She kept looking and then, with an almost physical jolt, it hit her—the person arguing with the policemen was Lilly. Gentle, soft-spoken Lilly was arguing with the cops. Jennie stared. Impossible to believe, but that was definitely Lilly. Who else was six feet tall, with hair down to their waist? *Something's really wrong.* Jennie put her hand on the door, tempted to rush over.

"Mom!" Tommy interrupted, indignant as only a wronged nine-year-old can be. "You said there was nothing more to see."

She figured distraction was the best defense. "Guess what. We got a new vending machine. I think it has bigger candy bars than the old one."

Andy asked, "Does it have Reese's Peanut Butter Cups?"

"Only one way to find out."

Fortunately, the machine was well stocked with Andy's favorite. Jennie fed in the required coins, then turned to Tommy. "How about you?"

He chewed on his lip and glared at her.

She said, "Look, I don't know any more than you do. We were out there together. You saw as much as I did. And there's no way we're going back."

Tommy finally announced he wanted a plain Hershey bar, no nuts.

She watched the kids bite into their candy, felt guilty, and said, "Why don't you ask Mrs. Harley if she can spare a glass of milk?"

Tommy countered, "You could buy us a Pepsi."

"You already got a candy bar. Don't push it." To ward off further argument, she added, "Go gather up your stuff and we'll hit the road. Meet me in Woody's office."

Woody was in the medical records room, a space used as an on-site office for doctors who visited Riverview. He half-sat, half-leaned on a desk, staring into space, long legs stretched in front of him, restless fingers beating a tattoo on his thighs. His grim expression did not change into its customary good-natured smile when Jennie entered the room.

"What happened?"

He repeated the terse answer he had given the boys. "Some people got sick."

"That explains the ambulance. Why the police cars?"

"Looks like they were poisoned."

Chapter Two

On the ride home, Tommy kept up a steady stream of questions. "Somebody got poisoned at Lilly's?"

Jennie maneuvered her classic VW Bug (christened "The Big Tomato" and referred to as TBT after a recent bright red paint job) around a monster Suburban before she answered. "I think he meant food poisoning." *What else could it be? But Woody sure didn't want to talk about it. Why? What if?* Jennie struggled to keep her own questions at bay so she could concentrate on Tommy's.

"Is food poisoning murder?"

"Of course not. It's an accident."

"But if somebody—"

Andy interrupted with a more personal concern. "Can we stop at McDonald's?"

She started to say no, thought about the takeout stir-fry she'd planned to get from Lilly's, and changed to,

"Okay." *It's getting late and I don't even know what's in the fridge.*

At bedtime, hoping to put the evening's events out of the kids' minds, she let herself be talked into an extra chapter of *Harry Potter*. The ploy worked. Even flashing lights, sirens, and police cars can't compete with life at Hogwarts. After she turned out their light, she kicked off her shoes, removed her slacks and sweater, and slipped into a favorite robe, then headed for the kitchen and a cup of tea.

She punched in Riverview's phone number while she waited for the kettle to boil. The receptionist answered, quietly professional with no hint of any disturbance in the neighborhood.

"Hey, Karen, it's me, Jennie. Know any more about what happened at Lilly's?"

"Uh uh. Police are still over there. At least they were ten minutes ago when I looked out."

"Is Woody around?"

"No. He left about half an hour ago. One of the cops came over. They talked for a few minutes. Woody took off right after."

"How about the residents? Are they aware of what happened?"

"I don't think so. There was a program in the dining hall. Some button-down insurance salesman scaring everybody about changes in Medicare. Almost everyone went."

"I forgot about that. Call me if you hear anything. Okay?"

"Sure."

Jennie said good-bye, hung up, and tried to figure out what to do next.

I'll call Lilly. She dialed the number and listened to the unanswered rings. Finally, the answering machine kicked in and she settled for leaving a message. "Hi. It's Jennie. I saw the excitement in the parking lot. Just wanted to check and see if you're all okay. Give me a call when you get a chance. If there's anything I can do, you know I'm here."

She considered calling Woody, but decided against it. There was no reason to think he'd be more willing to talk now than he'd been earlier.

She glanced at her watch. Another hour till the news. She wandered to the bookcase and took out a Carl Hiaasen. She stared at the pages for an eon that the clock registered as five minutes, and decided the time would pass quicker if she kept busy. *Maybe a snack.*

She opened the refrigerator and reached for a plastic container. *Wonder what this is.* She eased the lid off and sniffed. *Probably best not to know.* The phosphorescent mass set off another wave of speculation regarding the incident in Lilly's parking lot. By the time the news came on, the refrigerator was an organizational marvel. The jumble in Jennie's head was a different story.

She settled into a corner of the deep sofa, tucked her feet under the robe, and half-listened to the anchors spiel off the lead-in teasers, their chameleon-like faces reflecting just the right emotion for each item. When that litany was finished, one of them said, "Tonight's big story is the tragic loss of two respected educators."

Jennie leaned forward as the camera went to on-scene footage.

First, there was a close-up of the banshee woman. With the help of the just-visible microphone, Jennie could decipher her cry: "You don't understand! That's my husband!" The camera panned to the back of the building and the reporter said, "In this restaurant tonight, Hillcrest Junior High School lost not only Leonard Atkinson, a popular teacher, but also, Phillip Jeffries, its long-time principal."

Poor Lilly. And Fleur. She goes to Hillcrest. She must know both of those men. Fourteen-year-old Fleur was the middle of Lilly's three daughters. Jennie thought back to earlier that evening, when she'd witnessed Jasmine climbing down the arbor and sneaking out. Had she been wrong? Could it have been Fleur? She dismissed that idea and concentrated on the TV.

The deep voice of the anchor asked, "Do we know what caused the deaths?"

The reporter said, "The police decline to release a statement at this time. However, they took the food remaining on the plates of the two men to the laboratory for testing."

"Do you know what the food was?"

"That information is not available." The reporter looked at her notebook, then back at the camera. "I talked to a couple who were sitting at the table next to Mr. Jeffries and Mr. Atkinson. They declined to be interviewed on camera, but said that Mr. Atkinson suddenly stood up. His body arched. He collapsed to the floor, and when he was removed by the paramedics . . . this is a direct quote—" Here the reporter looked at her notebook and read, "He looked like he'd been scared to death." She looked at the camera and continued, "A few minutes later, Mr. Jeffries, who had apparently gone to make a phone call, showed a similar set of symptoms. On his way back to the table, he collapsed and was put into the ambulance with Mr. Atkinson. By the time they reached the hospital, both men were dead."

"Do you know if the symptoms you just described are consistent with those caused by food poisoning?"

The reporter hesitated before she answered. "I spoke with one of the other patrons, a doctor, who asked that his name not be used. He said food poisoning is unlikely. It doesn't occur that rapidly. According to him, the speed and manner of collapse suggest a quick-acting poison. Possibly strychnine." She cleared her throat and looked into the camera. "I want to make clear this was observed by an onlooker. The police have so far not released a statement."

"Do they suspect foul play?

"They say it's too soon to speculate."

The anchor nodded, then asked, "The woman we saw earlier trying to get into the ambulance, do you know who she is? I think it's safe to assume the wife of one of the victims, but which one?"

"I don't know. She refused to be interviewed."

There was a commercial. When the news resumed, the two anchors went on to other stories. Near the broadcast's end, the older of the two said, "Recapping our lead story, Phillip Jeffries, principal of Hillcrest Junior High School, and Leonard Atkinson, a popular math teacher at Hillcrest, both died tonight while dining at Lilly's Place, a small restaurant on the northern outskirts of the city."

The next camera shot was of the scene that had taken

place earlier in Lilly's parking lot. Once again Jennie watched the second of the two gurneys being loaded into the ambulance, the woman with the hair falling into her face, the camera's slow panning of the crowd. She saw herself, flanked by Tommy and Andy. The three of them stood within the circle of the floodlights, staring at the deadly scene. *What kind of mother*—she braced herself, waiting for the phone to ring.

It did.

"Hi, Tom."

"I just saw you and the kids on—"

"I know."

"What were you doing there with the kids in the middle of the night?"

"First of all, it wasn't the middle of the night. Only about six-thirty, in fact. I drove one of our residents to the airport and stopped by Riverview on the way home. We were just leaving when it happened."

"Why didn't you just get them out of there?"

"I did. As soon as I could."

"It looked to me—"

"Okay. I admit I stuck around for a few minutes. I wanted to make sure Lilly and the girls were okay. But my kids—"

"Our kids."

"Okay, our kids . . . and I didn't deliberately expose them to some dreadful scene that's going to mark them for life. I'm not an idiot!"

"I didn't say—"

"You implied."

There was a long silence, a sound that could have been a deep breath, then, "Okay, Jen, I'm sorry. It's just . . . when I saw the kids . . . all those police cars . . . it shook me up."

"Okay. Let's start over." She paused for a deep breath herself. "It's your weekend. What time should I have them ready."

"How about if I just pick them up at school? We're making dinner for Maria, and I'll take them shopping with me."

Jennie suppressed her thoughts about the dinner for Maria bit and said, "You remember they have swim team practice, don't you?"

"It's on the calendar. The Y. Eight-thirty."

Of course, it is. Mr. Type A. "Don't forget Andy needs drops in his ears."

"I know."

"You have—"

"Um hum."

Those details taken care of, they said good-bye, ending on a more cordial note than they'd begun. Jennie was left to envisage her sons having dinner with their father and Maria. Maria Perotti was the very attractive brunette who lived in the apartment above Tom's, and whom he always introduced as a "good friend." Just how "friendly" they were remained a little ambiguous. At least to Jennie. Not that she cared of course. Jennie and Tom had been married eleven years, separated for a year and a half, with a divorce pending. As for Jennie's own love life, Weston Goodley, a police lieutenant from up north in River County, was eagerly knocking on that door. Jennie liked Wes, but, married at nineteen, she was enjoying her new-found independence too much to rush into anything.

The phone rang again.

"Jennie, it's me."

"Lilly!" Concern for her friend banished the lovely Maria from Jennie's thoughts. "How are you?"

"I've been better. I guess you heard what happened."

"Yes. Anything I can do?"

"Can you stop by tomorrow? I don't really want to talk about it over the phone."

As Jennie replaced the receiver, she thought back over her day, driving Nathaniel Pynchon to the airport, thinking how dull it would be with Riverview's chief troublemaker off in London. Wrong, wrong, wrong. Nature does indeed abhor a vacuum.

Chapter Three

"Lilly's is closed."

The statement shouldn't have surprised Jennie, but it did. Maybe it was the bald manner in which it was spoken. Leda Barrons was executive director of Riverview and not known for her sensitivity. Everyone, including Jennie, agreed she was perfect for the job. Maybe too perfect. Leda possessed the ability to focus on the large picture of "What's best for Riverview?" Whereas Jennie's job, at least by her own definition, was to see that individual needs weren't lost in Leda's big picture. That the two would clash was a given.

"So," Leda continued, "You'll have to cancel the tea."

"Uh . . . I know the restaurant's closed, but maybe the catering—"

"The catering service is part of the restaurant."

Hoping for support, Jennie looked to the other faces around the conference table. Only Chaplain Joe Langley met her gaze, and he didn't look sympathetic. Jennie refused to give up. "I can't disappoint my ladies."

Jennie's ladies were a half dozen residents who, once a month, enjoyed an afternoon tea, catered by Lilly, and served with all the fuss and folderol that the name implied.

Leda said, "Well, you'll have to find a different caterer."

"But it's tomorrow."

Leda adjusted her small, rimless glasses and looked down at her notes—a signal she was ready to move on.

Jennie rejected the first half dozen comments that came to mind and contented herself with, "I'll think of something."

Leda darted a skeptical glance her way, but did not insist that the tea be canceled. She looked again at her notes, scribbled something on one of the pages, then sat back and said, "We have a lot to go over today. Jennifer, we may as well start with you."

Jennie pushed the tea dilemma to the back of her mind while she presented her report, a list of planned activities and a recap of the past month's events. With that taken care of, she returned to the problem at hand, all the while maintaining what she hoped was an attentive façade.

Though she loved Riverview's citizens in general, this morning her concern was focused on one in particular, Doreen Tull. Doreen, one of the so-called tea ladies, had a unique relationship with Jasmine, Lilly's troublesome oldest daughter. Jennie knew she'd be devastated by the murders. With her co-workers' voices droning in the background, she flipped a mental coin: Lilly . . . Doreen. Who first? Lilly won the toss. *That way, I'll have something to tell Doreen when I see her.*

The meeting dragged on. Same old yada yada.

Afterward, Jennie went directly to Lilly's. She hesitated at the yellow crime scene tape, scanned the area, then ducked under and strode to the back door, trying to look like she belonged there. Though the main entrance was in front, Riverview people usually entered in the rear, through the kitchen. Today the door was locked. Jennie knocked, and while she waited for someone to respond, looked around. What had once been a sprawling flagstone patio with a magnificent view of the Mississippi, was now a crushed-stone parking lot. Across the alley, between the old house and the river, was Riverview Manor.

When no one answered Jennie's knock, she went around to the front. As she passed under the arbor, she thought of Jasmine disappearing over the railing. More yellow tape sagged across the porch steps. This time Jennie stepped over without bothering to look around. The building that housed the restaurant, once known as the Wainwright mansion, stood proud and lonely, with a cracked sidewalk running along its front and small cottages crouching near its flanks.

There was no response at the front door either. She put her hands to the sides of her face, peered through one of the narrow rectangles of beveled glass, and saw Lilly and her mother-in-law, Elizabeth Wainwright. A thick green ledger and an untidy assortment of papers lay on the table between them.

Lilly spotted her and ran to unlock the door. She greeted Jennie with a hug. Lilly was a tall woman, just a shade under six feet, and generously proportioned, rounded without being fat. Hair the color of mahogany flowed in waves to her waist. Dark eyes and brown skin revealed her Hawaiian heritage. Jennie knew that she had met and married Charles Wainwright when he was working as a mechanic at Kahului Airport.

Lilly said, "They closed us down, Jen."

"I know. Are you going to be okay?"

The elder Mrs. Wainwright, who did not rise to greet Jennie, said, "Of course we'll be okay." She spoke as though addressing a third-grade Sunday school class, chastening them for their doubt.

Lilly was less positive than her mother-in-law. She held out her hands, palms up, and rolled her eyes.

Elizabeth rose and walked stiffly up the graceful stairway, head held high. Sixty-three years old, she possessed a natural dignity, undiminished by years of genteel near-poverty.

Jennie whispered to Lilly, "Should I come back later?"

Lilly pitched her voice higher, apparently wanting her mother-in-law to overhear. "Don't worry about it. She's been trying to escape all morning." She pointed to the ledger and papers. When Elizabeth disappeared behind the door at the top of the stairs, Lilly plopped down in a chair. "We operate on a shoestring in the best of times. I don't know how long we can survive if they keep us closed. I'll have to start looking for a job." She looked and sounded bone weary as she added, "If worse comes to worse, we'll sell. That's what we were talking about."

Jennie protested, "Surely they'll clear this up before long."

Lilly picked up a checkbook and slapped it against an ample thigh. "A week is the most we can stay afloat."

"Did you count this in your calculations?" Jennie handed her a check drawn on Riverview's account.

Lilly glanced at the check, shook her head. "I can't do the tea. Even the catering—"

"Is closed," Jennie finished for her. She drew back her hand, refusing to let Lilly return the check. "But you've already shopped. So we owe you the money. Anyway, I don't want to cancel, so I thought I'd buy the food from you, and since we both know I'm not exactly a world-class chef, see if I can coax you into helping me prepare it."

"But—"

Jennie held up her hand. "We'll do the cooking at my house and transport the food to Riverview. That way the restaurant's not involved. You're just a friend, helping me out in a pinch."

"The health department may not look at it that way."

Jennie crossed her eyes and did a wigwag of her head. "Well, *they're* not invited."

The round face broke into a smile. Lilly waved the check like a flag. "This'll buy us another week."

"So now you're up to two weeks. Anything can happen in that time. And just in case it doesn't, I've got a little rainy-day fund."

"I can't accept—"

"Sure you can. I know you're good for it." Jennie pasted on a smile and tried not to think of her own precarious finances.

A sharp rap on the glass in the front door made them both jump.

After a quick look, Lilly groaned.

Jennie recognized the television reporter who had covered the story on last night's news. She put her hand on Lilly's arm. "Ignore them."

"I can't. They've already seen us." She headed for the door. "Those people will crucify me if they think I have anything to hide."

The young woman who entered was dressed in a periwinkle blue suit, had short blond hair, and cheekbones that cameras fall in love with. She held out her hand. "Jill Newton."

A large man with a loopy smile and a camcorder dogged her footsteps.

Not wanting to be caught on camera again, Jennie excused herself and wandered through the restaurant. The rooms were large and airy, the ceilings high. Golden oak floors glowed with a patina that only time can bestow.

An open staircase, long and gracefully curved, led to the second floor. A burgundy-colored cord used to mark the upstairs as off-limits to customers lay in a loose coil on the third step. In the area between the stairs and the front door was a counter with a cash resister. Restrooms were in the alcove under the stairs. Past the restrooms and hidden by a wall was another staircase, less gracious than the one visible from the public rooms. Behind these was the restaurant kitchen.

"Psst."

The sound came from the top of the main stairs.

Jennie looked up and saw Elizabeth leaning through the half-open door, her head tilted forward, as though listening.

When the older woman saw Jennie, she mouthed, "The press?"

Jennie nodded.

Elizabeth disappeared behind the door, but not before she was spotted by the bright-eyed Ms. Newton.

The reporter brushed past Lilly and bounded up the stairs. The burgundy coil on the third step snagged the heel of her shoe, giving Lilly time to catch up. "That area is private."

That didn't stop Newton. She hesitated only long enough to disentangle her heel and motioned for the cameraman to follow. When she reached the closed door at the top, she did at least have the decency to knock. There was no response. She turned to Lilly. "Was that Elizabeth Wainwright?"

Lilly said, "I'm the one you want to talk to. I manage the restaurant and oversee the preparation of food." She returned to the first floor and looked up, her expression bidding the others to follow.

Both reporter and cameraman remained poised on the landing. Newton said, "You're the daughter-in-law, right? You were married to Charles Wainwright?"

"Yes."

"What can you tell me about the incident involving your husband and Phillip Jeffries?"

Lilly lifted her chin and glared. "My husband's been dead almost ten years."

Newton looked back at the closed door for a moment, then descended the stairs. She stopped no more than a foot from Lilly and thrust the microphone in her face. "Did you know Jeffries expelled him from high school? Prevented him from graduating?" She pronounced the words slowly and deliberately, more an accusation than a question.

Newton's cohort was directly behind her; the camera lens pointed at Lilly, leaving her no escape.

Chapter Four

The portal to the family living quarters opened. Elizabeth Wainwright stepped through and closed the door behind her. "You wish to speak to me?"

Her voice was as soft as always, her manner as serene. Only her hands betrayed her. Jennie watched the movement of arthritic fingers, clasping and unclasping, twisting the ring on her left hand.

If the reporter took note of her prey's hands, she gave no sign. She said, "I understand you and your son once had a confrontation with one of the victims, Mr. Jeffries. Is that true?"

Elizabeth's chin went up. "That was years ago."

Jill Newton said, "Nineteen to be exact."

"Such a silly thing. I'm surprised anyone remembers."

Newton smiled, but persisted. "It was important enough for the papers to print the story."

Elizabeth said nothing. Her fingers continued their restless dance.

Newton said, "Can you tell more about it?"

There was a moment of absolute silence. Jennie thought she saw fear in Elizabeth's blue eyes. She looked around to see if anyone else noticed. Hard to tell. She did see the red light on the camcorder, indicating that the scene was being documented.

Elizabeth joined the others on the first floor, swept past them, and led the way to a table. "We may as well be comfortable." After seating herself, she said to Lilly, "Perhaps you could make some tea."

The cameraman turned toward Lilly and Jennie.

Fleeing the red light, Jennie followed Lilly to the kitchen. "Do you know what she's talking about?"

She sighed. "Yes, but I can't imagine it has anything to do with what happened last night." She took cups and saucers from a cabinet and put them on a tray, then turned back to Jennie. "Listen, I need a favor."

"Sure. Anything."

"Can you drive Charly to swim practice for me tomorrow? I'd have Jasmine do it, but she's so undependable lately . . ." She finished with a plaintive shrug.

Jasmine and Charly (more formally, Charleen, named for her father, who had died before her birth) were the eldest and youngest of Lilly's three daughters. Jasmine, at sixteen, was giving her mother fits. Charly was a nine-year-old tomboy, whom Jennie's eldest son was not ashamed to call his best friend. The middle daughter, Fleur, at age fourteen, served as buffer between these two volatile personalities.

"Of course. You know I love having Charly around. I'll take her, watch the practice, then bring her home with me. You can pick her up when you come to help me get ready for the tea."

By the time they returned to the dining room, Elizabeth, Ms. Newton, and the cameraman were seated at one of the larger tables and were chatting, stiffly polite.

Jennie noted that the camera light was off.

"Thank you, dear." Elizabeth nodded at her daughter-in-law. "We waited for you. I told Ms. Newton I wanted you to hear anything I have to say." There was no visible dent in her perfect manners. Even her fingers were now controlled.

Lilly set the tray on the table.

Elizabeth played mother and did not speak until everyone's cup was filled. Then, "As you discovered, Phillip Jeffries and I had a terrible row. It happened years ago when my son, Charles, was a senior in high school. It was spring. Near graduation. Charles decided to play a little prank on Phillip, who was then vice-principal of the high school." She spoke in a formal, remote tone.

Ms. Newton interrupted. "As vice-principal, he was in charge of discipline. Right?"

"Yes," Elizabeth said, then went on, "Charles, along with some other boys, removed the engine from Mr. Jeffries' car and placed it in the school's front flowerbed. They replanted the petunias to frame the engine." She stopped, seemed to suppress a smile, which she promptly replaced with a frown. "I don't condone his actions, of course, but I still believe everyone over-reacted. I doubt the newspapers would have even picked it up if it hadn't occurred when nothing much was happening." A hint of anger crept into her voice. Her cheeks were a bright pink.

The red camera light glowed.

The reporter asked, "For this, your son was not allowed to graduate?"

"As I said, other boys were involved. When Charles refused to identify them, the administration decided to make an example of him."

"What did you do?"

"I went to Phillip . . . Mr. Jeffries . . . we had gone to school together. I tried to reason with him."

"Mrs. Jeffries said you threatened his life."

"Nonsense."

"After the incident your son left town. You wrote a letter to Mr. Jeffries saying that, because of his actions, you'd lost your only son. You said you were alone in the world, and you hoped someday the people he loved most would know that feeling."

"That's a far cry from threatening to kill him."

Lilly interrupted. "Why are you dragging this up now?"

"Mrs. Jeffries called. Told me about the letter. She interpreted it as a threat and has never forgotten it."

"Rosalyn Jeffries always was one to hang on to a grudge. But nineteen years is ridiculous. Even for her." Elizabeth favored Ms. Newton with a frosty smile. "I believe I've answered your questions." She rose and headed toward the staircase.

Jennie was surprised that Newton offered no argument.

After the newspeople left, Lilly relocked the front door and invited Jennie to join her in the family quarters.

At the top of the stairs was a large open space, which

served as a living room. One wall was broken up by a series of doors leading, Jennie knew, to the bedrooms and the former sunroom, which had been converted into an eat-in kitchen so the family would have a space separate from the restaurant. Each of these rooms had a french door leading to the porch that ran along the rear of the building.

Lilly waved Jennie to a chair. "Give me a minute, okay?" She went to Elizabeth's door at the far end of the line, tapped gently, then went in.

While Jennie waited for Lilly to return, she studied the framed school pictures and snapshots of the three girls. All shared their mother's dark coloring and almond eyes, but their manner of presenting themselves could not have been more different.

Sixteen-year-old Jasmine wore her hair short, gelled, and spiked. In her left ear there was a row of silver studs that stretched from the earlobe up past the curve of her ear; a single large silver loop dangled from her right ear. Jennie knew Jasmine was frequently in trouble at school, most often for cutting a class or blowing off an assignment. The one class she never skipped was art. Into that she poured the passion she withheld from the others.

Fourteen-year-old Fleur wore her hair long and loose, so that it seemed to float around her. She almost always wore a dress or skirt and at least half a dozen jangling bracelets. Her school record was as different from her sister's as her appearance. She made good grades, was popular with both teachers and students. In short, Fleur was the kid all the adults loved.

And then there was Jennie's favorite, Charly, the baby of the family. Most of the photos showed her in

T-shirts and jeans or shorts, with her mop of unruly hair pulled into a ponytail.

Lilly came back, shaking her head.

"Problems?" Jennie asked.

Lilly shrugged. "Who knows? She refuses to talk. Sometimes she's worse than Jasmine."

Jennie gave Lilly's shoulder a squeeze. "Wish I could stay, but I have to get back to work."

"Don't worry about it. What time do you want to pick up Charly tomorrow?"

"About eight."

"Good. I should be at your house by ten. The tea's not till two-thirty, so we'll have plenty of time."

"Sounds good." Jennie turned to go, remembered Lilly's earlier remark, and asked, "You aren't really thinking of selling?"

Lilly hesitated. "We've had an offer. A generous one."

"Anyone I know?"

Lilly nodded, then said, "Well, know of her, anyway. Constance Barlow." When Jennie looked blank, she added, "Mid-South Historic Preservation Society."

Jennie's mind flashed back to the night before, the distinguished-looking woman she'd seen scanning the crowd while others watched the gurneys being loaded into the ambulance. So that's who she is. "When did she make the offer?"

"A week or so ago."

Jennie couldn't hide her surprise. "You didn't even mention it."

"No reason to. We said no."

And now you may be forced to sell.

* * *

Back at Riverview, Jennie went directly to the dining room. As usual, the tea ladies had staked their claim on the best location—a table near the sliding glass doors overlooking the courtyard. When Jennie arrived five chairs were occupied. The sixth was empty.

Georgia Peterson, self-appointed spokesperson for the group, waved Jennie over. "Doreen's in her room."

Jennie asked, "Isn't she coming to lunch?"

"She said she's not hungry."

"I'll go talk to her."

"I'd leave her alone if I were you."

Doreen was the most recent addition to the tea ladies' circle and, at sixty-seven, the youngest. She'd lost the use of her legs in a cycling accident three years ago and used a wheelchair to whiz through Riverview's corridors.

Before the accident, Jennie knew Doreen had been an unusually active person. She'd never married, had focused instead on her career as an artist. In addition, she'd been an avid hiker and cyclist, activities she spoke of often and with undisguised longing. Fortunately, she was still able to use her hands and could continue her painting.

Jennie stared at the gothic-lettered plaque on the closed door: *Please Do Not Disturb. Working On a Masterpiece.* Small foxes curled sinuously around the letters, softening the words' impact without diluting their meaning. When Doreen wanted company, she left her door open and reversed the sign, stating: *Come On In—Always Ready for a Good Gossip.* An assortment of whimsical avian creatures fluttered around the edges of this message, clutching teacups in claws that resembled the fingers of the other tea ladies, right down to the rings they wore.

In ordinary circumstances, Jennie would not even consider knocking if the *Do Not Disturb* side showed. Today, however, she was concerned about Doreen's reaction to last night's events. Though she presented a sunny face to the world most of the time, Doreen was subject to bouts of depression, and Jennie was afraid the murders at Lilly's would send her spiraling into a dark spell.

Since Lilly catered most special events at Riverview, she and her girls were known to everyone who lived or worked there. Residents and staff universally loved Lilly and the two younger girls. Few felt the same about Jasmine. Doreen was among those who did. She seemed to identify with the rebellious sixteen-year-old and had become her mentor and defender.

Jennie steeled herself and disobeyed the sign. When there was no response to her knock, she said, "Doreen, it's me, Jennie."

Still no answer.

"May I come in?"

"Can you read?"

"Yes. I'd like to talk to you though."

Silence.

"Please, Doreen. I need your advice." Seconds passed. Jennie waited, whistling softly to signal her continued presence. Finally, she heard a listless, "Okay." She slipped through the door and closed it behind her.

Doreen was a large woman, with a homey, generous look about her. Normally, her demeanor invited the sharing of secrets. Not so today. Today it said *No Tres-passing.* Loud and clear. Wisps of pewter-colored hair hung limp around her face and dark circles underscored her hazel eyes. More alarming, her hands were idle, her fingers splayed on the arms of her chair. Most people reveal themselves through their eyes, or the small lines around their mouths. The key to Doreen was her hands. They were well formed, with long, square-tipped fingers, usually in motion, like a moth seeking light.

The sight of Doreen's inert fingers sent a wash of sympathy through Jennie. "Are you okay?" she asked.

The older woman answered Jennie's smile with a fierce scowl. "You said you need my advice."

Jennie took a second to regroup, then said, "It's about Jasmine."

Doreen lifted her chin and met Jennie's gaze.

Jennie was having second thoughts, but knew there was no backing away now. "I saw her sneak out of the house last night. It was about six-thirty, when all the excitement was going on. She climbed over the porch railing and down the arbor."

"How do you know it was her?"

"Who else would it be?"

Even Doreen didn't contest this. "Do you know where she went?" Her fingers began to show signs of life, as she tightened her grasp on the chair. Her expression dared Jennie to offer bad news.

"No. There was a lot going on, and I had Tommy and Andy with me. I lost track when she climbed over the railing."

"This is what you want me to advise you about?"

"I haven't told Lilly yet."

"Why not?"

Why didn't I? Jennie looked around the room, drinking in its richness, while she tried to answer the question for herself.

Most walls in Riverview were a predictable off-white. Doreen had insisted that hers be painted a deep gold, bordering on orange. Against this backdrop, she displayed her own pictures—abstract works with swirling lines and sumptious colors.

"I don't know. I intended to when I saw her this morning, but she was already stressed about being closed down, worrying about money and how they'll survive. Then, a reporter came by and started asking questions about some ancient conflict between Elizabeth and one of the victims." Jennie hesitated, trying to find words to articulate her reason for not telling Lilly about her daughter. "It seemed, you know, too much."

Doreen began fussing with her hair, using the beautiful fingers to tuck it behind her ears. "Try not to worry about it," she said. "I'll speak to Jasmine. Maybe we can spare Lilly. I agree she doesn't need anything else on her plate right now."

"Thanks. If Jasmine'll listen to anyone, it's you." Jennie reached for Doreen's hand and held it between her own. "I came here today because I thought you'd be upset and—"

"Oh, you mean your plea for advice was a trick to gain entry to my sanctuary?" There could be no missing the teasing mockery in Doreen's voice.

Jennie laughed. "Well, actually I did need the advice. But I admit I came here with the intention of helping you. And you end up doing me a favor."

"As it turned out, it's a favor to me, too. Took me out of myself."

Jennie kissed her on the forehead and turned to go. Halfway to the door, she stopped. "Are we doing the right thing? Not telling Lilly, I mean."

Doreen tilted her head and half smiled. "Can anyone ever be sure of that?"

The question remained in Jennie's head for the rest of the day, as impossible to banish as an off-key nursery rhyme. And about as helpful. Right now, Jennie needed a direction, not another maze.

Chapter Five

Promptly at eight on Saturday morning, Jennie pulled up in front of Lilly's Place. She gave the horn a light tap and waved when Charly appeared on the porch, followed by her grandmother.

Elizabeth glanced toward the car and returned Jennie's greeting before she turned her attention back to Charly. She fiddled with the top button of the little girl's raincoat, then pressed an umbrella into her hands.

Charly squirmed away and ran down the steps to the car. The deep violet of the umbrella and vivid yellow of her slicker were the only bright spots in an otherwise bleak day.

Jennie greeted her with a cheery, "Good morning."

Charly's tepid "Hi" was such a departure from her usual buoyancy that Jennie reached over and ran a finger over the curve of a rain-spotted check. "Maybe not so good after all," she said, "unless you're a duck."

The child responded with a dutiful smile.

Jennie was at a loss for what to say next. She pushed the button on the radio, switching from jazz to her kids' favorite rock station.

Charly didn't seem to notice.

She's really down. Not surprising. Two people murdered in her own home. "Want to talk about it?"

"About what?"

Jennie chose her words with care. "I understand you're upset. Anybody would be."

"I'm tired of talking about it. That's all anybody thinks about."

They lapsed into a silence broken only by the twitchy, insistent sound coming from the radio. The music ended and an aggressively upbeat disc jockey promised to be right back after the news. Four commercials later, a newscaster launched into an account of the murders. "Police have confirmed that the deaths of two educators were caused by strychnine poisoning. Strychnine is the poison used to kills rats and is readily—"

Jennie reached for the button.

Charly was quicker. The child twisted the dial. In the quiet that followed, she sat staring straight ahead, jaw clenched, tears streaming down her face.

Instinct told Jennie to let her cry. When they pulled into the Y parking lot, Jennie said, "There are tissues in the glove compartment."

Charly helped herself to a tissue, blew her nose, and whispered, "Thanks."

Jennie went with Charly to the changing room and made sure the coach was there, then headed for the gallery. The pool at the Y was new—ten lanes wide,

Olympic-sized, with a glassed-in viewing loft. The smell of chlorine penetrated even there. Spectators clustered in small groups throughout the area. Jennie chose an isolated spot and scanned the children lined at the pool's edge. She smiled, forgetting Charly for the moment, when she spotted first Tommy, then Andy. They were at opposite ends of the pool, each busy with his own age group.

A tall shadow appeared. Tom.

He sat on the bench next to her, so close their shoulders were almost touching. "We need to talk."

Without looking away from the kids, she said, "So? Talk."

"Did something happen the other night you didn't tell me?"

Shouts of other parents echoed off the too-bright, tiled walls. Jennie tilted her head closer to hear above the tumult. "Like what?"

"Anything."

His serious tone cut short the flip response she started to make. She thought a moment before she answered. "Nothing except what you already know."

His expression prompted her to reiterate. "We went outside. Police were all over the place. The ambulance—"

"Tommy's obsessed with these murders."

"What do you expect? He's nine-years old. It's TV come to life."

"There's more to it than that."

"How do you know? What'd he say?"

He hunched his shoulders. "Nothing really. He just seems, uh, I don't know, strange."

"After what's happened, I'd be worried if he didn't act strange."

Tom gave her that look, the one that meant, "Get serious."

She asked, "Did you talk to him about it?"

"I tried. He shut me out." Crinkly lines around his eyes showed how much this hurt.

Jennie noted his pain and tried to sooth it. "It's not you. He'll talk when he's ready. I'll try, too, but if we push too hard, he'll clam up more." When the lines didn't disappear, she added, "He's like you, you know."

Pleasure showed in Tom's eyes, but he kept his answer light. "A hopeless case, huh?"

"You said it. Not me."

They laughed together and watched their kids without speaking again until it was time to go. Then, while they were putting on their coats, Jennie said, "I'll talk to Tommy. See if I can get him to open up."

"You'll keep me posted?"

"Don't I always?"

He did a wibble-wobble of his hand before he headed down the narrow, tiled corridor to the boys' locker room.

Jennie watched, then turned in the opposite direction to get Charly.

The ride home was too quiet.

Jennie tried to break the ice. "I watched from the viewing area. You were awesome. Especially in the butterfly. I never could master that stroke."

"It's not really that hard." Charly's words were barely audible.

"Not if you're a born champ." Jennie reached over to touch her cheek. "Wouldn't be surprised to see you in the Olympics some day."

No response.

Stop. You're trying too hard. Jennie made every effort to follow Charly's lead and didn't say more. When the silence became oppressive, she switched on the radio. "How about a little music?" Angry lyrics exploded from the dashboard area. "You like this?"

Charly shrugged.

"Mind if I change it?"

Jennie pushed the button for the oldies station and was relieved to hear the upbeat sound of an old Beatles' tune. "We all live in a yellow submarine," she sang along, smiling an invitation to Charly to join in. No such luck. The song over, the announcer's voice came on: "And now for the news: The police are continuing—"

This time it was Jennie who turned off the radio. She looked at Charly, expecting to see more tears.

The little girl's eyes were narrowed to slits, but dry. The delicate bones of her jaw were rigid. "Mr. Atkinson was a bad man. He deserved to die!"

Jennie felt her heart constrict. *What did she mean by that?* She started to ask, but Charly's face warned her not to. Unbidden, the image of Jasmine sneaking over the porch railing came to mind.

"Will Tommy and Andy be home pretty soon?" Charly asked when they pulled into the Connors' drive.

"No. They're with their dad until after dinner tomorrow."

"When's my mom gonna be here?"

"About fifteen minutes."

The time was 9:45 and Lilly had said she'd be there around 10. The fifteen minutes stretched to half an hour. Longer. No Lilly.

Charly glued her nose to the window and stared out at the driveway.

Jennie tried to distract her. "Want to help me get ready for your mom?"

"Okay." The reply was sluggish but, Jennie figured, better than nothing.

When Charly joined her in the kitchen, Jennie gave her a spray bottle filled with cleaner and a sponge. "Let's see if we can have these counters spotless when she gets here."

That took all of two minutes. And so it went: Jennie kept inventing chores to at least keep Charly's hands busy. The little girl never refused a task, but it was clear her mind was elsewhere. Probably in at least six different places.

When they finally heard the slam of a car door, Charly was out the door like a beagle after a bunny.

Jennie knew the child needed a few minutes alone with her mother so she waited inside. She glanced at the clock. Eleven ten. More than an hour late. *Something's happened.*

Apparently Charly thought so, too. Her high, sweet voice carried into the house. "Where were you?" "Is everyone okay?" "How's Jasmine?" She stopped and looked directly into Lilly's face.

That's what she really wants to know.

Lilly's answer was not discernible.

Jennie remembered the slender figure on the porch

and Doreen's promise to talk to Jasmine. *I hope we're doing the right thing.*

When they came through the door, the usually independent nine-year-old was clinging to her mother's hand like a shy toddler. She released it only when Lilly wiggled out of her coat.

Jennie took the dripping garment from Lilly and said to Charly, "Mind putting that in the laundry room for your mom?" When she was gone, Jennie laid a sympathetic hand on Lilly's shoulder. "Sure you want to do this? I can probably muddle through on my own."

"And risk another poisoning?" Lilly's tone was light, but stress showed in the lines around her mouth.

Charly was back before Jennie could respond.

Lilly gave Jennie a look that signaled, "We'll talk later."

Jennie asked, "Charly, do you want to watch a video?" She pointed to the gleaming countertop. "You've already done your share here."

There was a vigorous shake of the head.

She's not leaving her mother's side.

Lilly said, "Okay, Button, but if you stick with us, you have to help. You know I don't allow idle hands in the kitchen when I'm cooking." She pulled a can of pineapple from a bag and handed it to Charly. "Here. Start by opening this. There are two more in the bag. Open them, too." She looked at Jennie. "I know. I hate using canned, but fresh pineapple in Memphis in February—" She rolled her eyes at the ceiling. "Besides, after an hour in my marinade, you'll never know the difference." She removed a thin, greenish bottle from another bag and set it on the counter.

"What—"

The doorbell interrupted. Jennie turned to Charly. "You mind getting that, honey? If it's Girl Scouts, tell them I've already ordered my cookies from you."

Lilly shook her head. "It may not be Girl Scouts. Charly, you stay here and get that pineapple open."

Surprised by this response, Jennie went to the door herself.

Another surprise—Ward Norris. Sharply creased chinos showed beneath his L. L. Bean jacket. Rain beaded on the tops of shiny tassel loafers.

He pushed his way into the house without waiting for an invitation. "Lilly here?"

Norris was a pharmacist, owner of the largest independent drugstore in the area, and, at least according to local gossip, much better off financially than his conservative lifestyle would indicate. He was good looking in the sense that there was nothing *bad* looking about him. He was of average height, not quite fat, but with the beginning of a paunch threatening to spill over his belt. His hair was dark blond, slightly wavy, and combed straight back from a narrow forehead. His eyes were distorted, magnified by the thick glasses he wore.

"Hi," Jennie said.

He ignored her greeting and asked again, "Is Lilly here?"

Before Jennie could answer, Lilly appeared. She said to Jennie, "I'll handle this."

Jennie took her at her word and went back to the kitchen. Charly sat on a high stool stirring pineapple chunks into a clear liquid. Jennie said, "Looks like you've got things under control. Any idea what I should be doing?"

Charly pointed to a packet of nuts lying on the counter. "You can chop those. Mom likes them in really little pieces."

The two of them worked side by side, with the sounds of angry whispers reaching them from the living room.

Jennie knew Ward had been a childhood friend of Lilly's husband, Charles. In the years since Charles' death, Ward had elected himself Lilly's protector and, Jennie knew, had aspirations of being much more. She'd listened to Lilly's accounts of his many proposals and her consistent refusals. Only the presence of the child kept Jennie from creeping closer to listen. She tried to make conversation to distract the little girl. "So, everything okay at school?"

"Um hmm."

Lame question. Lame response. She searched for a topic that would divert the nine-year-old's attention from the argument in the next room.

"No!" Lilly's voice abandoned the whispered hiss. There was no doubting her anger.

"You're wrong. It's time."

"You have no right—"

The spoon clattered to the floor, and Charly bolted from the kitchen.

Jennie followed.

Lilly stopped mid-sentence. Both she and Ward turned to look at Charly.

Jennie may as well have been on another planet for all the notice they gave her.

Chapter Six

After Ward left, Jennie looked at Lilly, waiting for an explanation.

Lilly stood motionless, staring at the door, her mouth clamped tight.

Unable to bear the silence, Jennie attempted a laugh. "That's a side of him I've never seen before. I thought he was just a guy who filled pill bottles. Meek and mild."

Lilly finally spoke. "Nobody's that simple."

"I know, but—"

Lilly didn't allow her to finish. She grabbed Charly's coat from a chair and held it out. "Come on, Button. Time to scoot." To Jennie, she said, "Everything's almost ready. Just follow my directions." She pointed toward the kitchen, where three index cards lay on the counter. "Then all you have to do is take the food to Riverview and set up. I'm sure you can find someone there to help you."

"How about you?"

"I can't be involved. Not with my place closed."

Lilly opened her purse and shifted items around. She snapped it shut, then looked around the room, everywhere except at Jennie.

She can't say anything in front of Charly.

Jennie smiled at the little girl and said, "Your gym bag and your Gramma's umbrella are in the laundry room. Why don't you run and get them?"

When she was out of earshot, Jennie turned to Lilly. "What's going on?"

"I'm kind of in a hurry. Ton of things to do." Lilly pulled up the hood of her raincoat, shielding her face.

"That's it?" Jennie stepped closer, so she was directly in front of Lilly and her face was no longer hidden. "Come on, you know you can trust me."

"I'm sorry I was late. We had an unexpected visitor." The struggle for composure was evident in Lilly's voice and in the way she jammed her hands deep into her pockets. "Constance Barlow dropped by." She hesitated, apparently listening for Charly's return before she continued, "She renewed her offer to buy. Even upped the price." Another pause, then, "That only took a few minutes. But I had trouble getting away from Elizabeth. The property's in both our names, and we both have to agree for a sale to go through."

"She doesn't think you'd sell?"

"That's the problem. She knows I won't."

"I thought—"

"I know you did. But you've got it backwards. Barlow wants to turn our place into an upscale bed and breakfast. 'Return it to its former glory,' is how she puts it. And she's sold Elizabeth on the idea." She turned to face Jennie. "I don't blame Elizabeth. Barlow said she'd hire a PR person to write up a family history, really play up all the good stuff, how the Wainwrights helped found the community. What noble muckety-mucks they were. Elizabeth misses being part of the social scene. To make matters worse, Ward had to butt in—."

"What's he—"

Charly came back and stood between her mother and Jennie.

Lilly buttoned her daughter's raincoat and pulled the hood up over her hair. "Ready to go?"

Charly nodded.

Jennie noted the closed look on her friend's face and moved to safer ground. "I'll call after the tea, and let you know how it went."

"Fine." With that, Lilly slipped past Jennie, out the door.

Negotiating the winding road to Riverview, Jennie couldn't get the argument between Lilly and Ward Norris out of her mind, nor the fact that Lilly so obviously hadn't wanted to talk about it. In addition, she'd come to the conclusion that it wasn't fair to ask Doreen to deal with Jasmine.

I have to tell Lilly myself. Jeez, I hate to do it now, though. She's already on overload. Maybe it's better to let Doreen handle it. No, that's not fair. I'm the one who saw Jasmine sneak out. I'm the one who should deal with it. Would she tell me where she was going if I asked her flat out? It's worth a try. The thing between Lilly and Ward . . . maybe it has something to do with the murders. Probably not. He'd never go that far. Anyway, it's none of my business. But why does it matter to him if she sells?

These warring thoughts were like so many ants, scurrying through the labyrinth in Jennie's brain. To still them, she said aloud, "I'll find a way to help Lilly and not bug her about the other stuff. She doesn't need anybody else on her case."

With that resolution, Jennie pulled into the parking lot and looked around for someone to help her with the food trays. She didn't have to look far. An aide was slouched on the steps, curls of smoke rising from a cupped fist. *Incredible that anyone working in health care would smoke.* She waved, motioning him over.

He nodded, took a long drag, dropped the cigarette, and ground it under his heel, before unfolding his lanky form.

After she put the food in the refrigerator, she checked her watch. *Great. I have time to talk to Leda.*

Riverview Manor was laid out as a large rectangle with an expansive courtyard filling the central area. The executive director's office and the activities room were directly opposite one another. On nice days, Jennie cut through the open area to reach the office. Today, she took the longer route, through the corridors.

Leda was squinting at her computer monitor. Classical music accompanied the click of manicured nails on the keyboard while Leda hummed along.

Jennie paused at the threshold of the open door and listened, but didn't recognize the piece. Something Russian. Lush and romantic. She smiled to herself and reflected, not for the first time, that Riverview's tough majordomo had a soft side. *Too bad she keeps it so well hidden.*

Jennie tapped on the door frame. "Have a minute?" she asked when the older woman looked up.

Leda stopped humming. "Yes," she said.

"I've been thinking. I know Lilly can't cater any of our events until this mess is cleared up."

Leda's eyes became wary.

"But what if she taught a quilting class? A small one, just to my tea ladies. They could each pay her, say a hundred dollars. That would give Lilly something to live on and keep them busy at the same time."

The six women who made up Jennie's tea ladies could easily afford to pay for Lilly's services. In addition to being financially independent, they were intelligent, restless and, if left to their own devices, prone to stir up trouble. Jennie was pretty sure Leda would jump at this plan to keep them busy and dead sure they would jump at the chance to do something a cut above the usual arts and crafts.

"Have you talked to them about it? Or Lilly?"

"I wanted to clear it with you first."

Leda looked doubtful, so Jennie leaned a little harder. "Hawaiian quilts. Taught by a real Hawaiian. That's something I bet no other retirement community has done. We might even get a write-up in *Golden Years*."

Jennie took the gleam in Leda's eye for a yes and left before she could change her mind.

Okay. On to the next hurdle. Back in the activities room, she searched through the stack of yellow Post-its in her top drawer for the one with Jasmine's cell phone number. *I know I have it somewhere.* Three slips from the bottom, *Yes!*

Jasmine answered on the first ring. Jennie heard loud music and laughter in the background and surmised that the girl was in a car with friends.

"Jasmine, this is Jennifer Connors. We need to talk."

"Yeah, well right now, I'm—"

"I don't mean now. This afternoon."

"Sorry. I can't—"

"I have something to ask you."

"So, ask."

"This has to be face to face." When there was no response, Jennie added, "I'd like to speak to you before I go to your mother."

"What are—"

"I'll be free this afternoon by four o'clock. Here at Riverview. You know where to find me."

"I'm not—"

"Just be here." With that, Jennie hung up. *Let's hope she shows.*

Chapter Seven

After making the date with Jasmine, Jennie rearranged a few pieces of furniture to make the spacious room cozier for the tea. She moved two small square tables closer to the windows, pushed them together to form a single rectangle, which she covered with a damask cloth. That done, she took a minute to admire the view through the sliding glass doors.

A massive oak spread its limbs over dormant flowerbeds and a patio. The rain had diminished to a fine drizzle that blurred images and created a ghostly scene.

A husky voice intruded. "Penny for your thoughts, young lady."

The voice belonged to Georgia Peterson. She was carrying a shallow wicker basket filled with primroses in deep purple and creamy white.

"Georgie, that's lovely."

"Does that mean you're not sharing your thoughts?"

Jennie laughed. "Believe me, they're not worth even a penny."

"People always say that when they have secrets to keep." Georgia was the oldest and most wickedly inquisitive of the tea ladies. She was close to ninety. Just how close she refused to divulge, saying, "A lady never reveals her age or her bank balance." She looked frail, but as everyone at Riverview knew, this little old lady was made of solid steel. She might decline to answer personal questions, but she never refrained from asking them. According to her, it was a privilege earned by longevity. "So, do you have secrets to keep?"

Jennie ignored the probing. "The primroses are lovely. Just the thing for a dreary day."

Georgie lowered her eyes with insincere modesty and set the basket on the table.

Doreen arrived next and maneuvered her wheelchair into position to inspect the centerpiece. Doreen was Georgie's opposite in every way except mental toughness. The two of them jockeyed relentlessly for leadership of the group, a conflict both enjoyed.

Frances Lavery, Faye Dodd, Tess Zumwalt, and Vera Sanborn completed the half dozen. They entered the activities area as a group a minute or two after Doreen and joined her at the table.

Georgie remained a little apart, allowing the others to study the flowers. The women took turns providing a fresh centerpiece to grace the tea table and were fiercely competitive in this endeavor. Tea time usually began with a brutal critique of the table decoration. Today, however, everyone was too excited about the murders at Lilly's to put their hearts into the routine.

Frances Lavery tried. She fingered a primrose petal and said, "Georgie, is this supposed to represent the path you've traveled?"

Georgie huffed a little, but laughed along with everyone else.

Frances was a former English teacher, who kept her wit honed by a constant reading (and re-reading) of Jane Austen, a habit she tried to instill in the high school students she tutored one afternoon a week.

Jennie listened to the good-natured teasing while she arranged food and dishes around the centerpiece. She tried to gauge Doreen's mood without blatantly watching her.

If Doreen was still in the dumps, she hid it well. "At least the basket will come in handy," she said with a sidelong glance at Georgie.

Jennie did not share in the conversation until Georgie sidled up beside her and asked, "Have you talked to Lilly today?"

"Yes, she helped me with this. Unofficially, of course."

"What did she have to say about the murders?"

Tess Zumwalt, a former FBI agent and the group's quietest member, leaned a little closer, but said nothing.

Jennie kept her answer as brief as possible. "We talked about other things."

Georgie was not about to be put off. "How about Jasmine? Where was she while all this was going on?"

The last question brought on a chorus of sighs and clicking of tongues until Doreen stopped it. "Don't tell me you're going to say Jasmine had anything to do with those killings. A girl has a little spirit, and she gets blamed for anything that goes wrong. You're all jealous of her." Red patches glowed in her cheeks and her fingers punched holes in the air.

Vera Sanborn tried to calm her down. She lifted the primrose basket to eye level. "Nice healthy plants. Where'd you get them, Georgie?" Vera had been a landscape designer and had a common-sense approach that usually managed to bring Georgie down to earth. This time it didn't work.

Georgie took the basket from her and slammed it back on the table. "Don't change the subject!"

Jennie stepped in. "Look what Lilly made for us. Let's forget about murders and such and enjoy the food."

Everyone except Georgie looked grateful. She looked ready for a good fight, but she headed toward the table with the others.

Jennie nodded at Faye Dodd, signaling her to say the blessing.

Fay Dodd was a retired minister and the ethical center of the group.

When the amen had been spoken, Doreen said, "With all the hubbub, I almost forgot. I asked my niece to drop by. Jennie, do you mind?"

"Of course not."

Faye swept her arm over the table. "There's enough food here for a Methodist picnic."

Doreen said, "She's a vice-principal at the school where Phillip Jeffries was principal." She paused, then added with elaborate casualness, "She'll be the acting principal for the rest of the year, or at least until they name a replacement for Jeffries."

Jennie had the distinct feeling something was going on. She wondered about Doreen's motive for inviting her niece on this particular Saturday. Though they'd never discussed it with her, she knew the ladies had an unwritten rule that no outsider would be invited to the tea without the approval of all six.

When she didn't say anything, the ladies began to talk at once, pressing closer with each statement.

"Don't you see what this means?"

"She'll be very helpful to us."

Helpful? To us?

"She has access to all sorts of information."

Access? She studied their faces. *So that's it. They plan to investigate the murders.* Without acknowledging that she knew what they were talking about, Jennie tried to shift their attention by telling them about the proposed quilting class.

As usual, Georgia reacted first. "Yes!" She made a fist and pumped her arm, more in the manner of a NHL right-winger than a great-grandmother. "Lilly'll be here. That'll make it easier."

Before Jennie had a chance to tell them that she was not going to help them play detective, she heard Doreen say, "Hello, dear."

No one would doubt that the person entering the room was related to Doreen. She was tall, just a tad overweight, and shared Doreen's intense hazel eyes and wavy hair, though hers was dark auburn, while her aunt's was peppered with gray. Both had a wide, generous mouth.

Another woman hovered near the door, but did not come in. Jennie started to go over and see if she needed something, but was distracted when Doreen put a hand on her arm. "Jennie, this is my niece, Ann Tull."

Jennie reached out toward the newcomer. "I'm Jennie Connors. Glad to finally meet you. Doreen's talked about you so much, I feel I already know you."

"Ditto. If you promise not to believe everything she said about me, I'll return the favor."

"Deal."

Doreen interrupted. "I've been trying to get you two together, but Ann can only visit when she's not at school, and then, of course, Jennie's home with her boys."

Ann turned to the other ladies. "Good to see all of you again. Thanks for including me."

There were murmurs of welcome, all sincere, as far as Jennie could tell, then laughter from Ann. "Well, another little surprise. The invited guest brought an uninvited guest." She stretched her arm toward the doorway in a welcoming gesture. "Come on in, Martha. You can see this is a friendly crowd."

Jennie stared at the waiflike individual who came forward. It was the banshee woman.

Ann said, "This is Martha Atkinson. She, uh . . ." a pause during which Ann seemed to be deciding what to say next. "Her husband was one of the men who died Thursday night in Lilly's place."

The silence was palpable.

Martha nodded timidly. When she finally spoke, her voice was a squeek. "I just dropped by the school to get Leonard's things, and Miss Tull was kind enough to invite me to your tea." A slight pause, a nervous laugh, then, "I guess she thought I needed a distraction. I hope you don't mind."

Georgie was quick to take her arm and say, "Of course not. What a dreadful experience. You must tell us all about it. Talk can be so therapeutic."

Jennie noted that Martha flinched a little at Georgie's touch.

She's like a frightened child, Jennie thought, and tried to rescue her. "I think we could all use a cup of tea. Lilly found something new for us. Ginger peach. I haven't tasted it, but it smells heavenly. Georgie, will you pour?"

Never one to turn down a position at center stage, Georgie relinquished Martha's arm and began filling cups.

The other women gathered around Martha and insisted she sit in the most comfortable chair, a tall wingback in the center of the U-shaped arrangement. This made her easily accessible to their attention, welcome or not.

Then, it began. Questions from every side.

"Had your husband been at Hillcrest long?"

"No, we came here just before Christmas."

"The school year had already started?"

A timid nod confirmed that.

"Where were you before?"

"Up in River County."

"Did your husband like Hillcrest?"

Martha picked at a loose thread dangling from her sweater before she answered. "Very much."

"Did he find people friendly? Sometimes parents can—"

Jennie felt she had to intervene. "Mrs. Atkinson is—"

"Please, call me Martha."

Jennie smiled at her. "Okay." She turned back to the ladies, focusing on Georgie, the source of most of the questions. "Why don't we just let Martha enjoy her tea. I'm sure she's tired of talking about this."

Georgia was quick to answer. "Talking about traumas is—"

Jennie interrupted again, "Yes, at the right time. And that's up to Martha."

The beleagured woman looked at Jennie gratefully. "I guess I'm not ready for social gatherings." She turned to Ann. "Thank you for trying." Her hands were shaking when she placed her still-full teacup on the table and scurried toward the door.

Insistent voices followed her. "I hope you'll visit us again." "Remember, we're here if you need someone to talk to."

With Martha gone, Georgie settled herself in the wingback. She made no attempt to hide her displeasure with Jennie. "We just missed a golden opportunity. I don't understand you. Don't you care about justice?"

Jennie stood her ground. "Harassing that poor woman has nothing to do with justice."

Tess said, "If we find out who killed her husband, it has."

Georgie crumbled a macaroon in her plate. "All we did was ask a few subtle questions."

"About as subtle as a bear at a ballet," Jennie snapped.

Since Jennie rarely lost her cool, the ladies, even Georgie, quietly sipped their tea and picked at Lilly's pineapple salad. It didn't take long, though, for them to turn their attention to Ann.

"She seemed nervous, don't you think?"

"Who? Martha?" Ann sipped her tea and looked back at them with mild eyes.

"Yes." The ladies, except Doreen, answered in chorus.

Doreen watched, her face free from any expression Jennie could read.

Ann patted her lips with a napkin, then said, "Under the circumstances, I think she's holding up very well."

"What can you tell us about the circumstances?"

Ann seemed more amused than angry at the question, which she clearly did not intend to answer. She smiled over the rim of her cup.

Georgie was undaunted. "You're the principal now. Does that mean you'll be helping with the investigation."

"I doubt the police need my help."

"Since both victims taught at Hillcrest, the school must be involved in some way."

"I've already spoken with the police."

"What did you tell them?"

Another smile. "I really can't talk about it."

"But we might be able to help."

"I think they have everything under control."

"Maybe a different point of view."

"I have to respect the confidentiality of my position." With that, Ann Tull settled back in her chair, sipped her tea, and refused to add more.

Chapter Eight

Ann Tull continued to parry questions with polite nonanswers for another ten minutes before she glanced at her watch and rose from the chair. "I hate to leave such good company, but I have a couple of things to do this afternoon." She gave each of the ladies a hug, spending extra time with Doreen. "Bye, Aunt Dorrie. I'll call you later."

Jennie watched, then walked with her into the hall. She waited until they were alone to speak. "Sorry about the inquisition."

Ann shrugged. "No need to apologize. That was a cakewalk compared to some parent conferences I've had."

When Jennie returned to the activities room, she found the elderly women huddled around Doreen's wheelchair, whispering.

At the click of Jennie's footsteps on the tile floor,

everyone turned. Georgie came forward. "She's playing her cards mighty close."

Jennie looked past Georgie to Doreen. *How does she feel about the way they grilled her niece?* Doreen's face betrayed nothing. *Did she know this would happen? Is she manipulating the others to investigate? Why? To make sure Jasmine isn't blamed?* That made more sense than anything else Jennie could think of.

Georgie refused to be ignored. She thrust her face within inches of Jennie's and demanded, "Well, don't you think she knows more than she's telling?"

Jennie repressed her rising impatience. "Probably, but it's confidential. She can't talk about it, and frankly, I don't think she would even if she could." She paused to look into each face and focused on Georgie's before she went on. "And we're going to respect her position."

"Well, of course we are." Georgie was purring now. She seated herself and picked up a teacup, the picture of decorous innocence. "We wouldn't dream of asking her to do anything unethical. We'll form our own task force. It would be easier if we had her input, but we'll manage without it."

Task force? Jeez. Too bad we can't limit her TV. Jennie kept her voice level. "I doubt the police will welcome your help."

"You've assisted them with matters like this," Georgia argued.

"Right. Remember how unhappy they were about it. Besides, that was different. I was thrust into both of those cases. This time I have a choice. And I choose to mind my own business."

Doreen said, "What about Lilly? Shouldn't we be doing everything we can to help her?"

Jennie suspected the real question was, "Shouldn't we make sure Jasmine isn't blamed?"

Georgie couldn't keep still. "And what could be more helpful than putting this killer behind bars? We'd remove the cloud from Lilly's restaurant."

Tess backed up Georgie, something that rarely happened. "Might even save the life of the killer's next victim."

The trip into fantasyland was beginning to strain Jennie's patience. "And risk your own lives in the process? Forget it."

Rebuttals came so fast she couldn't keep track of who said what, but the ladies were united in their determination.

"We're grown women."

"We have a right to decide for ourselves."

"With all the years we've lived, we can outwit some young punk who decides to go around poisoning people."

"You'd be surprised at the tricks still up our sleeves."

Jennie laughed in spite of herself. She knew pointing out the difficulty was like saying "Double dare you" to one of her boys. "I don't doubt that for a minute, but I can't let you become involved in this. For one thing, I'd be joining the ranks of the unemployed." She stopped to look into each face again. "And I'd miss you guys like crazy."

That stopped them, but Jennie had no illusions that the victory was permanent. Hoping to divert their attention, she asked, "What about the quilt class?"

Georgia rolled her eyes.

Doreen stared out the window and drew looping figure eights on her chair arms with her beautiful fingers.

There was a collective groan from the other four.

Jennie tried to revive their previous interest. "You want to help Lilly? This could save her life. Her financial life anyway. And if we all avoid the subject of the murders, maybe we can distract her from her problems. That's worth something, even if it's only for a few minutes."

The ladies agreed to go ahead with the class. Jennie knew it was not the last she would hear of their plan, but at least the matter was put aside for the moment.

Jennie replayed the afternoon's events in her head while she loaded a cart with dishes. She hadn't been honest when she disclaimed interest in solving the murders. Her resolve to help Lilly was as great as theirs. She wondered if the ladies had noticed her perk up when Martha Atkinson mentioned River County? She glanced at her watch. Three fifty-three. *Seven minutes till Jasmine gets here. I just have time to make a call.*

The receptionist answered, "River County offices. How may I help you?"

"I'd like to speak to Lieutenant Goodley."

"Who's calling?"

"Jennifer Connors."

Goodley must have been close. Instead of the usual click, followed by canned music, Jennie heard, "It's for you, Wes. Jennifer Connors."

"Jennie." There was a definite lilt in his voice when he said her name.

"Hi. Just want to see if I can bring anything tonight."

"No. Everything's covered." He paused, added, "Sure you know how to get here?"

"I wrote down your directions. Sounds simple enough."

"So, see you around seven."

"Okay." She hung up and stared into the courtyard, watching two squirrels chase each other through the branches of the oak tree. Weston Goodley had become a part of Jennie's life when she and Tom separated. Wes, divorced with a daughter hundreds of miles away in Philadelphia, understood Jennie's conflicted feelings more than anyone in her apple-pie wholesome family. She enjoyed their dinner and movie dates, but this was the first time she'd been to his home, and it seemed to take the relationship a step further. *Am I going to regret this? Can't think about it now. On to the next problem.* That thought had hardly crossed her mind when the next problem swaggered in.

Jasmine was dressed in black from head to toe: black jeans, black turtleneck, black leather vest, black hiking boots that wouldn't have looked out of place on Everest. Her jet-black hair, formed into two-inch spikes, glistened with enough gel to pave the proverbial road to hell. Though Jennie doubted Jasmine had anything like good intentions. *Dressed to intimidate.* She kept this to herself and said, "Thanks for coming."

Jasmine dragged a chair over so the rear of it was turned toward Jennie's desk. She straddled the seat and sat with her arms crossed over the chair back. Her eyes met Jennie's. "So?"

It was a challenge, and Jennie knew there was only one way to meet it—head-on. "I saw you sneak out of your house Thursday night."

The girl looked surprised for a moment, then her

face assumed a tough, nothing-can-touch-me expression. "You're nuts."

Jennie ignored the remark and continued, "I watched you climb down the arbor."

"Oh? And what did I do then?"

"I don't know. I'd like to find out."

"I don't know what you saw, but it wasn't me."

"Let's not kid each other. I do know what I saw. I haven't said anything to your mother. She's got enough to worry about now. If you'll just—"

"I get it. I confide in you, promise to be a good little girl, and you," here the teenager paused to smile angelically before she went on in the sweet falsetto of a much-younger child, "won't tell my mommy." By the time the words were out of her mouth, her eyes were slits of pure malice.

Jennie tried again. "I'm not your enemy. I just want—"

"I know what you want. You want everyone to do everything you say. And you'll rescue my poor family from this awful mess. Well, we don't need to be rescued. Stay away from us."

"I can't keep this from your mother."

"There's nothing to keep from anybody!" Jasmine screamed her protest.

Jennie's peripheral vision caught several co-workers lingering in the hall just outside the activities room door. She took a deep breath and spoke softly. "I don't know—"

Far from following Jennie's lead and lowering her voice, Jasmine exploded. She bolted upright and knocked her chair into the cart. Cups and plates leaped into the air, descended in slow motion, and splintered as they crashed onto the tile floor. Jasmine shouted through the din, "That's right! You don't know! And you don't even know what it is you don't know!"

Jennie used every ounce of self-control to keep her voice level. "So tell me. If there's an explanation—"

Jasmine kicked the chair aside and backed toward the door, shards of glass crunching under her boots. "I don't have to explain anything to you."

"Okay. Then explain it to your mother." Jennie heard her own voice escalating. She stopped for a calming breath. "Jas, there was a double murder that night."

"And you think I did it."

"No, of course, not. But, for your own protection—"

"I don't need protection."

"Let me finish. What I'm trying to say is you need to be able to account for your whereabouts."

"I was in my room studying."

Jennie met her eyes and didn't answer.

"You think I'm lying?"

"As a matter of fact, I do. Your mother has to know this. And probably the police."

"Meaning you intend to tell them?"

"What choice do I have?"

It seemed to Jennie that some of the air went out of Jasmine, but only momentarily. After looking at her through narrowed eyes for a few seconds, the girl said, "Something could happen to you."

Jennie bit her tongue. *Don't let her get to you. She's a kid. Her own worst enemy.*

"I could make it happen. I have friends who know how to do all kinds of things."

"Jasmine, please—"

"Your house. This place. Anything could happen. Your car." Jasmine brought her face close to Jennie's and lowered her voice to an ominous whisper. "Think about that."

Chapter Nine

Jennie couldn't get Jasmine's words out of her head as she navigated the winding River Road to Weston Goodley's house. She'd witnessed enough of the girl's theatrics over the years that she didn't take them seriously—at least not as a danger to herself or her kids. A glimpse into the sixteen-year-old's state of mind, well, that was another matter. Something else to tell Lilly. *Your daughter threatens people and sneaks out of the house at night.* What a load to dump on a friend.

She was approaching Riverview now. Traffic was beginning to build up, unusual for River Road on a Saturday evening. She looked for an ambulance and sent up a silent prayer that nothing had happened to any of the residents. An unexpected shaft of light caught her eye when she passed Tailor's Lane, the street bordering the retirement community on the north. Colored lights played off the white brick wall of the dry cleaner across the street. A police car. A hundred yards ahead, she saw more lights, another police car, orange cones in the road. A cop funneled traffic into one lane. Fear seized her. An accident. Someone from Riverview? She came to a complete stop.

Brakes squealed. A horn sounded behind her. The cop's arm pinwheeled, motioning for her to keep moving.

She glanced in the rearview mirror and saw a hand raised in the familiar one-finger salute. She moved forward. Once past the accident scene, she reached for her cell phone, but drew her hand back and replaced it on the steering wheel when she neared a sharp curve. *River Road is no place to be driving distracted. I'll call when I get there.* By the time she reached Goodley's, she had convinced herself there was no reason to believe anyone from Riverview had been involved in the accident. It wasn't time for a shift change or anything like that. She didn't make the call.

The police lieutenant was renovating an old farmhouse. It was five after seven when Jennie pulled into the driveway, but already pitch dark on this February evening. A yellow bulb cast a fifty-foot arc in front of the house, illuminating the entrance and tidy piles of plastic-covered lumber. She maneuvered TBT past them and parked next to Goodley's gray Jetta.

He appeared in the doorway before she had the key out of the ignition. His tall, thin build was similar to Tom's. In silhouette, it would be easy to mistake one for the other. Jennie considered this as she picked up the pie she'd brought as her contribution to dinner. She'd heard that women are always attracted to the same type of man. Were Wes and Tom the same type? More important, was she attracted to Wes? She liked him and enjoyed his company, but, at least so far, there was no real spark. She'd been nineteen when she married Tom after a whirlwind courtship. That relationship had been all sparks—and look where it had led. So much for fireworks.

"Hi." Wes's face as he came down the porch steps was far different from his usual serious mien. His smile said, "Christmas morning."

Jennie offered the pie. "Hope you like peach."

"My favorite, but I told you not to bring anything."

"If I didn't, I'd never be able to face my mother. She says when you go calling, you should have to knock with your elbows."

"Old school, huh?"

"With the dinosaurs."

He accepted the pie, gave it an appreciative sniff. "You bake this?"

"Sure I did. And I had Lilly put it in one of her boxes."

The smiled slipped a little.

"Believe me, you'd rather have one of Lilly's pies than mine."

They entered the house and were greeted by the sound of Mozart and the aroma of onions. Goodley said, "Excuse the smell. I'm making you a genuine Philly treat." He led her into a room to the left. A wood stove, centered on one wall, was flanked by twin sofas, deep and many-cushioned. After he took her coat, he said, "Have a seat. I'm almost ready."

"Can't I help?"

"Thanks, but no. You just relax."

She settled into one of the sofas and looked around. It was obvious the room where she sat had once been a porch. Multipaned windows beginning three feet from the floor reached to the low, sloping ceiling on three sides, including the wall behind the stove. On this dark night, the panes of glass acted as mirrors and reflected back the brightly-lit kitchen where Goodley worked. He moved from the cutting board on the counter to the stove with a single efficient sidestep.

A huge aquarium rested on the surface of a wide counter separating the two rooms. Jennie said, "Tommy's been wanting one of these."

"It's a good hobby."

"I'm trying to hold off until he's a older and can take care of it by himself."

"Start small. Just a few fish. Add more when he's ready."

She watched the darting repetition in the glass cage. "Do you suppose they ever get bored?"

He laughed. "Somebody's probably done a study on that, but personally I never thought about it. Anyway, it's not something to discuss on an empty stomach." He motioned her to the table. "Bet you've never had a real cheesesteak."

"Sure I have."

"Not a Philly cheesesteak."

"There's a difference?"

"Of course. Every place has something they do better than anyone else. Memphis has barbecue. Philadelphia does cheesesteaks. And pretzels." He held out a chair for Jennie and when she was seated, sat opposite her.

Jennie lifted the top of the roll for a closer look. "Looks delicious."

"Let's hope it passes the taste test."

She waited until they were well into the meal before she brought up the murders. "I guess you heard about two people being poisoned at Lilly's."

"Um."

"Rat poison or something."

"Strychnine."

She realized his response hadn't been a question. "So you have heard about it?"

Another, "Um."

He wasn't making this easy. "How about the victims? Do you know them?"

Goodley finished his sandwich, pointed to Jennie's half-eaten food. "You don't like my cooking?"

"It's wonderful." She took another bite. "Tastes even better than it looks." She'd heard the warning in his voice but chose to ignore it and persisted in her questioning. "About the murder victims? Did you know either of them?"

He didn't answer.

She didn't give up. "One was from River County."

"I'm a transplanted Yankee. You think I know everybody who ever lived in this county?"

"No, but—"

"According to the paper, those guys were both teachers, law-abiding citizens. Not the sort of people I get to know." The words came out clipped and precise. His fingers beat a tattoo on the tabletop.

"Hear me out. One of them, Leonard Atkinson, came to Hillcrest as a replacement in the middle of the year."

"What's wrong with that?"

"He was highly recommended."

"So?"

"Why was he available on short notice if he was so good?"

"Money. Memphis has a lot more than a rural district like River County."

"I don't think it's that simple."

Goodley didn't roll his eyes, but he may as well have. He sat watching her with an infuriating half-smile.

She didn't give up. "Teachers don't make moves like that. They finish out their year, then move. Especially the good ones."

"What do you want me to do?"

"I thought you might've heard something about him."

"If I kept up on all the gossip in the county I wouldn't have time to do my job."

"But you could check it, couldn't you?"

"Check what?"

"I think there's something a little off in the way he left."

"Your reason?"

"I can't say exactly. It's just—"

"Intuition?"

The face of the man with whom she'd begun dinner had changed. Narrowed eyes and a half-smile told Jennie he thought she was a kook, meddling in affairs beyond her ken or worse, that she was cute, a little girl playing detective. She considered telling him about Charly's passionate statement 'Mr. Atkinson was a bad man. He deserved to die.' She couldn't do that without exposing the little girl to . . . what? Would Goodley feel compelled to convey the information to the investigators in Memphis? Of course. He was a cop. What would the Memphis police do? Question Charly? That was obvious. And the other two girls? Surely. Where might that lead? Would they question Jennie herself to find out more about the conversation? If that happened, she'd have to tell them she'd seen Jasmine sneak out of the building the night of the murders. Would the police make a connection between Charly's outburst and her older sister's action? Was there a connection? These things darted through Jennie's mind like the fish in Goodley's aquarium.

Goodley, once again the no-nonsense cop, continued to stare at her with an expression that was something between a smile and a challenge.

A challenge she had to meet. "Intuition. You say that like a four-letter word. You don't believe in it?"

A buzz interrupted before he could answer. A ringing cell phone. They exchanged glances.

Jennie said, "It's mine." She dug through the multitude of objects in the tote bag and found her phone in the bottom, wedged under her address book. "Hello."

"Jennie?"

"Yes."

"This is Faye." There was an unmistakable urgency in her voice. "Doreen needs you."

"What happened?"

Sounds of crying in the background blocked part of Faye's words. "Just come. Okay?"

"I'm up in River County. I'll be there as soon as I can. About half an hour."

"Okay." With no further explanation, there came a click signaling disconnect.

Chapter Ten

Jennie looked at Goodley, who was still seated and was watching her. "That was Faye Dodd, one of my ladies. I have to go."

"What's wrong?"

"I don't know. She just said to come right away. Something about Doreen."

"Who's that?"

"A resident I'm especially close to. I have to go. Thanks for everything." While she talked, she gathered her things.

He picked up a glove she'd dropped and handed it to her. "Sure you're okay to drive? You look a little shaky."

"I'm fine." She knew how rude it was to rush off in the middle of dinner, more important perhaps, in the middle of an argument, but there was no choice. Her concern for Riverview's people was second only to her love for Tommy and Andy.

* * *

Driving the narrow, curving road she tried to figure out what Faye's terse summons meant. Had Doreen had a heart attack? That seemed unlikely. Jennie wondered if she had slipped into a serious bout of depression. That was certainly a possibility. What could have triggered it? Just a few hours ago, she had been fine. Jennie thought back over the afternoon, trying to remember any nuance that might have disturbed Doreen's hardworn equilibrium.

No use speculating. I'll know soon enough.

She had no trouble finding a parking place on the side street. She glanced at the car clock as she turned off the ignition. Nine forty-five. Most of the residents would be asleep or getting ready for bed. She jogged across the lawn to the front entrance and went directly to Doreen's room. There she found the elderly woman sitting in her wheelchair crying silently. Faye sat on the edge of the bed, a box of tissues in her lap, stroking Doreen's arm.

Faye rose to greet Jennie, but it was Doreen who spoke. "Ann is dead." Those few words were all she could manage before she began to weep, great sobs racking her body.

It took Jennie a split second to realize that Doreen was speaking of her niece, Ann Tull. She crossed the distance between them in long strides, took Doreen's face in her hands, and touched her forehead to the other woman's, the closest thing to a hug the wheelchair would allow. Jennie had no idea how long they stayed like that, perhaps only a few seconds. It seemed a long time until Doreen pulled free.

She said, "An accident. That's what they said. The

brakes failed, and she didn't make the curve along the bluff."

"I'm so sorry. I know how close you were to your niece, how much you loved her." Even as she said the words, they sounded trite. Why is it so hard to express sympathy? Does death take us back to a place and time before words? A time when touch was used to say whatever needed to be said?

Inadequate as the words seemed to Jennie, they apparently reached Doreen. She made a visible effort to calm herself, accepted a tissue from Faye, and dabbed at her wet cheeks.

Jennie said, "Do you want to talk about it?"

Doreen nodded and reached for another tissue. "I feel responsible."

"You're not, of course."

Another nod. "I know that. Still—" Another sob overtook her.

Jennie stroked her hair and waited for her to regain control.

"She came back to see me."

"That doesn't make it your fault. She came because she wanted to be with you."

Doreen stared at the picture on her bedside table— a photograph of herself as a much younger woman, dressed in slacks and a turtleneck, holding the hand of a little girl who gazed up at her with worshipful eyes. Finally, she looked up at Jennie. "I called her after you left and apologized for the grilling we gave her. I told her I was proud of her for not answering our nosy questions, that she was right not to tell tales out of school."

Faye was still sitting on the bed. She hadn't moved since Jennie had come into the room.

Doreen reached out to her. "Thank you for being here. I don't know how I'd have managed without you."

Faye just nodded and turned to leave. When she passed Jennie, she said, "I'll be in my room if you need me."

Jennie remembered the police activity when she'd passed Riverview on the way to her dinner date. She wondered if it was connected to Ann's accident. She followed Faye out into the hall. "When did it happen?"

"The accident?"

"Yes."

Faye thought a minute. "Six-thirty, give or take a bit either way."

Nausea threatened to swamp Jennie when she realized she'd practically witnessed the death of Doreen's niece. *Buck up. You don't have time for this. Doreen needs you.* She took a minute to compose herself. *Ann was just leaving here. No wonder Doreen feels she's to blame.*

When Jennie went back into Doreen's room, she found her staring again at the photograph of her young self and the little girl.

That's Doreen with Ann, the closest thing she's ever had to a child of her own.

Jennie sat in a chair next to Doreen's work table. "She came back again?"

"Yes, we had dinner together." There was a long pause and straightening of shoulders before she went on. "An early dinner. Trays here in my room. She sat where you're sitting now." Doreen remained perfectly still. Only her hands moved, the beautiful fingers twisting and weaving around one another like willow catkins bowing to the wind.

Jennie said, "She came back because she loves being with you. She spent her last hour with someone she cares about. That's what you need to remember. The brakes would have failed the next time she used them wherever she was. It has nothing to do with you."

Doreen looked straight into Jennie's eyes. "I don't think it was an accident."

"But you said—"

The older woman held up her hand. "Hear me out. Ann was upset. I had the feeling she wanted to tell me something, but was holding back."

"What are you saying?"

"The murders at Lilly's. I think she knew something."

Jennie stared. It made sense. If anyone knew, Ann would be that person. She worked with both of the victims. And since stepping into the position of acting principal, she had access to all the records.

Doreen said, "She seemed ill at ease this afternoon."

"Really? I thought she was remarkably serene."

"But you don't know her."

Jennie had to admit the truth of that.

"Besides, I know she'd just had her car at the VW dealer for servicing."

A shiver went through Jennie, that feeling her grandmother called a goose walking over your grave. "VW?"

"Yes, she drove a little Bug, very much like yours."

"Was it red?" Jennie said, feeling stupid, but needing to be absolutely sure.

"No, black." Doreen met Jennie's eyes, and added, "Otherwise, just like yours."

Jasmine? No. Don't even go there. "Have you told the police about your suspicions?"

"No. It didn't occur to me at first. Then they were gone. Now I don't know what to do. It seems so outlandish." She was quiet for a moment. "I'll mention it to them. They should at least be aware it's something to be checked."

Jennie wondered if Doreen had heard Jasmine threaten her. Was that adding to her anguish? She had to talk to Lilly about her daughter. Soon.

Chapter Eleven

Jennie dialed the number, listened to the phone ring, and sent up a silent prayer that Lilly, not one of the girls, would pick up.

"Hello."

A prayer answered. A good start to a Sunday morning. "Hi, Lilly, it's me, Jennie."

"Kind of early, isn't it?"

"I wanted to catch you before you went to church."

"Oh." There were a couple of beats of silence before she added, "We're sort of hibernating this weekend." The tone was bitter, unusual for Lilly. But understandable.

Jennie didn't bother to voice this sentiment. "Yeah, I'm taking the day off too. The boys are with Tom. I thought I'd go for a jog along the river. Want to join me?"

There was another pause before Lilly answered. "You don't jog. What's up?"

"I need to talk to you."

"Just come on over. I'll give you breakfast."

"Uh, I'd kind of like to be somewhere away from the rest of the family."

"The girls are sleeping in. Elizabeth will go to church even if we don't."

"Please, Lilly, humor me. This is important."

A huge sigh. "Okay, but do we have to jog?"

"I'll let you set the pace."

Half an hour later, Jennie pulled into the restaurant parking lot. A blue jay squawked when she stepped out of the car. "Good morning to you too." She fluttered her fingers in a wave when he flew away. Feeling foolish, she glanced around, hoping no one was watching. Not a soul in sight. She noted that the crime scene tape was gone and speculated that the police must have finished their search of the grounds. *Wonder if they found anything.*

Lilly appeared, carrying a canvas tote.

"What's in the bag?"

Lilly held it open. "Thermos of coffee and some scones."

"Great idea."

The two women crossed the alley without further comment, skirted Riverview, and waited for a break in the traffic on River Road. Their destination was the bike path, a five-foot-wide strip of macadam that ran along the bluff, used by bikers and joggers, as well as those who preferred a more leisurely pace. From this vantage point, the river spread before them, a broad, undulating ribbon of café au lait—the muddy Mississippi, old man of legend and song. The sky was brilliant, the air balmy, the kind of February day you count as a gift in west Tennessee.

Jennie took a minute to savor the grandeur of river and sky, inviting a measure of their ancient wisdom to enter her soul. She'd spent a sleepless night worrying how to tell Lilly about her daughter and hadn't come up with anything. The fact that more than two days had passed since she'd spotted Jasmine creeping along the porch and disappearing down the arbor didn't make the chore any easier.

Lilly broke the silence. "So? What's on your mind?"

Jennie hesitated.

"As if I didn't know."

That caught her off-guard. "What do you mean?"

"You want to know about Ward. What we were fighting about."

"No, that's not—well, yes I do, but I know it's none of my business. There's something else."

"Oh?"

She blurted it out. "Jasmine. Thursday night, I saw her on the porch. She was flat against the wall, like she was hiding. After a minute, she climbed down the arbor."

Lilly stopped. She grabbed Jennie's arm, bringing her to a halt also. "What're you talking about?"

"The night of the murders, the kids and I ordered takeout for our dinner. When we went to pick it up, police and ambulances were all over the place. Everything was happening at once. They had the parking lot cordoned off and wouldn't let us in. We stayed a few minutes before we went back to Riverview. While the ambulances were being loaded, I happened to look up. That's when I saw her."

"You're sure?"

"Yes. Although when I asked her—"

"You asked *her?* Why didn't you come to *me?*"

This was what Jennie had been dreading. How to explain that one? "You had so much on your mind, I thought maybe she'd tell me where she went and if it didn't seem important, I could spare you at least one worry."

Lilly set the tote down on the path, put her hands on Jennie's shoulders, and looked straight into her eyes. "I'll be the judge of what's important where my daughters are concerned. Okay?"

"I knew you'd be upset."

"You wouldn't be?"

Jennie resisted the impulse to turn away from the fury in her friend's eyes. "I'm sorry. I know it was wrong."

Lilly looked ready to argue more when suddenly the fight ebbed out of her. She sat down on the edge of the path, put her elbows on her knees, and buried her face in her hands.

Jennie eased down beside her and put an arm around her shoulder.

A pair of middle-aged joggers approached. The man almost tripped over the tote. The woman made a scolding remark that Jennie didn't bother to answer.

She retrieved the bag, unscrewed the thermos, and smelled its contents. Lilly's special blend, a fragrant mixture no one could resist. She poured a generous serving into the metal top and held it so the aroma reached Lilly. "Here. This might help."

Lilly raised her face from her hands. "It's going to take more than a little coffee."

"At least it won't hurt."

Lilly took a tentative sip, another, and seemed to draw strength from the mundane action. She closed her eyes momentarily. "What next?"

Jennie felt rotten for being the one to deliver this latest blow and tried to soften its impact. "When I talked to Jasmine, she denied it. Maybe she's telling the truth."

"With Jas, anything's possible. The problem is, how will I know?"

"Maybe when you talk to her, you can get her to tell you exactly what happened."

"Is that what you tried to do?"

"Yes. Obviously, it didn't work." Jennie shivered. It might be a beautiful day, but it was still February.

"You need some coffee too." Lilly set her own cup on the path and reached into the tote bag. She brought out an earthenware mug and handed it to Jennie. While Jennie poured her coffee, Lilly unwrapped two blueberry scones from a linen napkin. "My girls have a saying, 'When all else fails, bury your troubles in carbs.' "

"You have very wise daughters."

Lilly sighed. "They're good kids. But sometimes, it's just, you know, too much."

"Don't beat yourself up. You're a great mother. Not a bad daughter-in-law either. What would happen to Elizabeth if you didn't take care of her?"

"I don't know, Jen. Right now, I feel like I'm the captain of a sinking ship and everybody's going down with me."

"Hey, remember, it's always darkest before the dawn."

"Now there's an original thought."

"How about, it's an ill wind that blows no good?"

"Try again."

Jennie came up one dreadful platitude after another until they were both laughing. Some of Lilly's giggles sounded ominously close to sobs, but Jennie figured it was at least a start.

Another jogger came by, this one with an inquisitive beagle in tow. The dog made a beeline for the tote bag, which Jennie just managed to rescue. The owner was a jovial sort, who saluted and excused his pet.

Jennie waited until he was out of earshot. "Want to talk? I admit I don't have any answers, but maybe if we put our heads together, we can think of something."

Lilly puffed her cheeks and blew out the air. "You don't know how good it is to be with someone who doesn't think they have all the answers. Everyone else thinks they know exactly what I should do. And they won't give me a minute's peace to think it out myself. Ward's the worst." There was a long pause. "What am I going to do, Jen?"

"About what?"

"Cut it out. You know what."

Jennie said, "He wants to get married and live happily ever after. Right?"

Lilly nodded.

"Some might not consider that a bad thing."

"But my girls—especially Jasmine."

Jennie spoke carefully. "Do you really want to let her make that decision? That's a lot of responsibility for a kid."

Lilly straightened up and glared at Jennie. "I thought you were the one person who'd understand."

"I do. Or at least I did, but lately . . . I'm getting the

feeling you're ready to move on, and you're hanging on to Charlie's memory because . . . I don't know . . . because you don't know what else to do."

Lilly stared at the river and let the tears run down her face.

Jennie put her hand on Lilly's arm. "I'm sorry. I had no right to say that."

It was a long half minute before Lilly said, "It's okay. You could be right. Ward's . . ." She stared at the pulsing water as though spellbound by the current. Finally, she looked up and met Jennie'e eyes. "He's always just . . . been there."

Jennie saw the pain in Lilly's eyes and said, "You don't have to talk about it if you don't want to."

"I do want to. I've never talked about it to anyone. How could I? It started right after Charlie died. The next day, as a matter of fact." Lilly sat quietly, as though gathering memories, before she spoke again. "Charlie and Ward were best friends, had been since grade school. Different as fire and ice, but close as brothers. Both were only children. Both lost their fathers when they were small. Charlie was reckless. Ward was, well, you know him. From what I've heard, even when he was a little kid, he was careful. Never took chances." She paused to look at Jennie. "Not like our kids, huh?"

"Unfortunately, no." Jennie laughed.

Lilly laughed with her and went on, "Charlie, on the other hand, couldn't take enough. He loved speed. Before he was old enough to drive, he was tinkering with engines. The older kids brought their cycles and cars to him to fix. And he did. Elizabeth discouraged him, tried to push him into something she thought was dignified."

Jennie said, "Sounds like her."

Lilly nodded. "Even if Charlie hadn't gotten kicked out of school, he'd have run away. Anyway, that's what he said. He wanted to see the world. So he left home and got a job in a garage somewhere in Oklahoma. Kept working his way west until he ended up in Hawaii. By that time he was a top-notch mechanic. He got a job fixing airplane engines at Kahului. That's what he was doing when I met him. And we got married. He was only nineteen at the time. I was twenty-one. A year later we had Jasmine. Then Fleur." She stopped to watch a circling hawk.

Jennie waited quietly.

After a few seconds, Lilly spoke again. "Then Charlie decided we should come back here. We moved in with Elizabeth. It was supposed to be temporary, but, well, you know how those things go." Lilly spread her hands and held them out to catch the sun. "Elizabeth needed us. I mean really needed us. She had no money. No skills. And you know how proud she is. The house was falling apart. Little by little we fixed it up."

Jennie had a sketchy knowledge of these things, which had happened before they'd met, but she felt Lilly's desperation to tell someone about them, to lay out her life for examination, not for her listener, but for herself. Her job as Lilly's friend was to make it easy.

She asked, "When did you open the restaurant?"

"After Charlie died. It was the only thing I could think to do. Two women. Two little girls. Then I found out I was pregnant."

"Must have been tough."

"That's putting it mildly. I wasn't sorry, though. That I was pregnant, I mean. I thought the baby was a gift." Lilly turned to look at Jennie. "I wanted to die myself when Charlie was killed."

Jennie could think of no response to that.

Apparently Lilly didn't expect one. She went on, "It wasn't even a real race. He was trying out a new car. It spun out of control. Hit a wall. He was killed instantly." She looked off into space. "That's what they kept saying. Instantly. He didn't suffer. He was the most alive person I've ever known. Then he was dead. Instantly. How is that possible?"

Jennie pulled Lilly closer. They leaned against each other, shoulder to shoulder, each supporting the other.

"Ward and I were both watching. We followed the ambulance to the hospital. But we both knew it was too late. The girls were at home with Elizabeth." A huge gulp, then she went on, "Thank God for that. I had to go home and tell them. Ward went with me. He was almost as upset as I was. He took Elizabeth aside and told her. I told the girls." She stopped to wipe a tear from her cheek, then went on, "They were so little. Jasmine was six; Fleur had just turned four. Babies really."

"I can't even imagine how awful it must have been."

"Nobody can. Anyway, Ward was like a rock for all of us. The next day, he went to the funeral home with me."

"You don't have to talk about it."

Lilly looked at Jennie again. "But I do. This is the first time in all these years I've been able to."

"Not even to Elizabeth?"

Lilly shook her head. "She couldn't talk about anything concerning Charlie without bursting into tears. I couldn't either. We tiptoed around it like we were walking on eggshells, scared to death the girls would bring it up. They never did."

"Ward?"

"He was as bad as Elizabeth. Maybe they talked to each other. I don't know. They never mentioned Charlie's name around me. I think they were waiting for me to collapse. But I didn't. I kept myself together for the baby. When she was born, I named her Charleen after Charlie."

Jennie asked, "When did Ward, uh . . ."

"Not for a long time. He was married at the time Charlie died. He and his wife had a little boy a couple of months older than Fleur. It's funny. Even then, he spent more time with my kids than his own."

"Sounds like he was already in love with you."

Lilly waved the suggestion away. "No, no. That's not it. His wife was protective of the little boy. Hardly let him out of her sight. Ward didn't have a chance to be close to his own son."

"Did he try?"

Lilly hunched her shoulders. "I don't know."

"Were you friends with her? Ward's wife, I mean."

"Not really. My Charlie couldn't stand her. Said she was a control freak. Between the two of us, I thought they were too much alike to get along. Anyway, I never got to know her very well. She was strong-willed. I know that."

A low-pitched horn interrupted.

Jennie and Lilly looked toward the river and returned the wave of the tugboat captain.

"Poor man," Lilly whispered.

"Poor? Why?"

"Must be a lonely job."

"He has his crew."

"But the responsibility . . ." Lilly's voice drifted and her eyes remained fixed on the tiny vessel pushing a string of barges ten times its size. They rode low in the water; their progress upriver was painfully slow.

Jennie knew how heavily Lilly's own responsibilities weighed, but resisted the impulse to comment. Instead she gave her friend a backrub and waited for her to speak again.

"They got divorced about four years after the accident. Todd, that's Ward's son, was eight. Ward . . ." She stared at the river and didn't finish.

"He's crazy about you."

Lilly shrugged. "I'm not sure if he really wants me, or if he just wants to be Charlie. He always looked up to him. I know he wants to be a father to Charlie's kids. My kids. Like he wasn't allowed to be to Todd."

"Put like that, it sounds a little creepy."

"Yeah, maybe. He says he'll do anything in the world for me. These past few days—" She paused to look after the tug. "Sometimes I think he's almost glad about the murders. That I had to shut down, I mean. Like he thinks now I'll have to turn to him."

"That *is* creepy."

"I know. But on the other hand, maybe I'm wrong. Maybe he does love me. And to tell the truth, he'd make a better father than Charlie ever was." She paused to look at Jennie and managed a small smile. "If you tell anybody I said that, I'll deny I even know you."

Jennie laughed. "Your secret's safe with me." After a minute, she asked, "Anything left in the thermos?"

Lilly tipped the cylinder over the cup. Two drops came out. "Not enough to do anybody any good."

Jennie rubbed her hands together. "I'm getting cold just sitting here. Shall we walk or are you ready to go back?"

"Let's go back. Those scones are long gone. How's a hot breakfast sound?"

"Maybe not heaven, but close enough."

"Okay. Everybody'll be up now. We can have something to eat. And I'll talk to Jasmine. See what she has to say for herself. I'd like you to be around in case she tries to deny it."

"She's already denied it to me. I doubt she'll change her story."

"Right. It's not like her to back down."

Chapter Twelve

They climbed the hill from the path and crossed the road in companionable silence. When they passed Riverview, Jennie said, "I should stop in and see how Doreen's doing."

"Now?" Lilly's dark eyes were pleading. "You know you'll get stuck. It'll help if you're there when I talk to Jasmine."

Jennie hesitated, torn by conflicting loyalties. At the moment, Lilly's need was greater. "I'll call."

Jennie watched Lilly unlock the back door, then followed her past the restaurant kitchen. A chill snaked down her spine when she glanced into the usually bustling space. This morning it was dark, quiet, dominated by the hulking shapes of the commercial stove and refrigerator. A faint antiseptic odor wafted out instead of the fragrant bouquet of Lilly's unique South

Sea spices. Remnants of yellow crime scene tape still fluttered from the door frame.

Lilly passed with her head held high, eyes straight ahead. There was no acknowledgement of her domain's altered status. Neither spoke as they ascended the staircase leading to the family living area. The aroma of coffee drifted down.

Jennie wrinkled her nose in appreciation. "I think the girls are already working on breakfast."

"At least they've got the coffeepot on. Good thing." Lilly swung the canvas tote with the thermos. "This is bone dry."

Jennie concurred. "I know. We even drank the proverbial last drop."

Charly's anxious face greeted them when they entered the kitchen. "Mom? Where were you?"

"Jennie and I took a walk. I left you a note." Lilly set the thermos in the sink and ran water into it. She bent to kiss the top of her youngest daughter's head, then reached for Fleur, who was busy stirring eggs into a thick, golden mixture.

The preoccupied teenager leaned her cheek to be kissed without looking away from the mixing bowl.

Lilly asked, "Where's Jasmine?"

"Still asleep, I guess. She hasn't come out of her room yet."

"Okay." Lilly mouthed a silent, "Wish me luck," in Jennie's direction and left the kitchen.

Jennie gave her arm a quick squeeze when she passed by.

Fleur continued to stir the batter. Charly pulled a tall

stool near the counter where her sister was working and climbed on. Jennie remained in the doorway, apart from the family tableau, and watched.

From down the hall came the sound of a light tap on a wood door.

No response.

Another tap, this time louder, firmer.

"I thought you said we could all sleep in this morning." Jasmine sounded more grouchy than sleepy.

"It's after ten. Time to get up. We need to talk."

There was the sound of a door opening, closing, Lilly's soft tones, then an explosion of words. "And you believe her!" Within seconds, Jasmine burst into the kitchen. She stopped in front of Jennie and grabbed the front of her jacket. "I told you to stay away from my mother."

Jennie resisted the temptation to respond in kind. She kept her voice level. "You know I couldn't do that."

"No, of course not. Miss Goody Two Shoes has to make everything right." Jasmine removed her hands from Jennie's coat and spun away, almost colliding with Lilly, who had followed her into the room.

"Jasmine, stop! You can't blame Jennie for what she saw. She's not responsible for your actions."

"What actions? I didn't do anything. I was with you in the kitchen for a little while before I went upstairs. After that, I stayed in my room and studied. Even with all the police cars and everything. Why do you believe her instead of me? Your own daughter?"

Her outraged fury struck Jennie as that of a person wrongfully accused. *But I saw someone sneak off that porch. And it had to be Jasmine. Who else could have it have been?* She turned to Lilly and said, "Someone was creeping along the balcony the night of the murders," then to Jasmine, "If it wasn't you, there was an intruder. We'll notify the police. Maybe they can figure it out."

Jasmine flounced to the far end of the room and stood looking from Lilly to Jennie and back again. "Did she tell you I threatened her?"

Lilly responded by turning to Jennie.

Jennie said, "We didn't go into that."

"Into what?" Lilly faced Jennie. Her tone was accusing. "You still haven't leveled with me, have you?"

Jennie sighed. "She was angry. I didn't take everything she said seriously."

"I guess now you do, huh? Do you think I had Miss Tull's car fixed?" Jasmine's tone was ominous.

"No, of course not."

"Maybe I did."

Lilly went to her daughter and tried to embrace her. "Don't even say things like that."

Jasmine shook off her mother's arm and stalked away. "Why not? What difference does it make what I say? You don't believe me anyway." She began to pace, moving back and forth through the room with long, swift strides. She was wearing an oversized T-shirt, black, with an upraised fist printed on the front, paired with flannel pajama bottoms adorned with Cupids and pink hearts. Even in this incongrous combination, the girl projected an aura of defiant élan.

The only sounds for the next minute were the scrape of Fleur's spoon on the bowl and Jasmine's bare feet slapping the linoleum floor.

Fleur broke the spell. "Batter's ready," she said, "and the griddle's hot."

Charly bumped herself off the stool. "I'll set the table."

Jasmine started to leave.

Lilly put a hand on her shoulder and pushed her toward the table. She said quietly, "No. You're not going to your room. We're all going to have breakfast together and sort this out."

Jennie glanced at her watch.

Lilly said, "You're part of this too."

There was no arguing with that. "Okay, but I have to call Riverview. Tom's flying to Seattle this afternoon, so the kids'll be coming back early. He's bringing them to my office about eleven." She removed a cell phone from her jacket pocket. "I'll leave a message so he knows where I am. I can check on Doreen at the same time." She stepped out of the kitchen, away from the distraction of the Wainwright-family troubles.

By the time Jennie had completed her phone calls and joined them for breakfast, differences had been put aside in deference to food. Lilly and Jasmine were seated at opposite ends of the table, each of their faces devoid of obvious emotion.

Jennie paused in the doorway and studied them. Despite the absence of angry words, a funnel shape of tension hovered over the room. A restless tattoo of fingertips on the tabletop gave Jasmine away. Lilly's posture was too perfect, her manner too controlled to be genuine.

Jennie placed her hand on the back of an empty chair. "This anyone's special spot?"

Charly said, "That's Gramma's place, but she won't be home from church till later."

Jennie sat down and looked toward Lilly for a cue on how to proceed.

None came.

Fleur and Charly seemed determined to preserve the precarious calm. Fleur hovered over the griddle, deftly flipping the golden disks. Charly bustled from the stove to the table, setting filled plates before her mother, sisters, Jennie, and finally placing one for herself. Seconds later, Fleur joined them, saying, "Okay, dig in. They're no good cold."

Charly pushed a slender brown bottle toward Jennie. "Want some coconut syrup?"

"It smells heavenly." Jennie tipped the bottle over the stack of pancakes.

"Careful," Lilly warned. "A little goes a long way."

She took a small bite. "Umm. Fantastic. Can you buy this around here?"

Lilly poured a thin stream over her breakfast before she answered. "I've never tried, but I don't think so. My sister sends it. Part of our Christmas care package."

They managed to get through the meal with no fireworks. No one mentioned the earlier dispute. Jasmine stopped drumming her fingers and sat slouched over her breakfast, one elbow resting on the table, affecting exaggerated boredom, not joining in the conversation.

Lilly darted a series of disapproving glances toward her oldest daughter, but said nothing.

Everyone ate slowly, as though to prolong the respite. When pushing the fork around her empty plate became absurd, Jennie rose and began gathering dishes. "I'll head the cleanup crew."

"In a minute," Lilly said. "First, we have to settle

this. Jasmine, I want to know where you went that night."

"I told you. I didn't leave my room."

Fleur said, "That's right. I know she was there. I was with her."

Jasmine shot her sister a quick look, opened her mouth, but closed it without saying anything.

"Me too. I was there too," Charly said.

The three girls sat uniformly straight, looking their mother squarely in the eye. It was clear they were sticking together. And equally clear, at least to Jennie, that they were lying. But why?

Lilly looked from one impassive face to the other and finally said, "Okay, you girls are excused. Jennie, I'll take you up on the cleanup offer."

"Sure. Least I can do." She didn't know if she felt more relieved or concerned that further confrontation had been avoided, or at least postponed. The matter was not settled, but she couldn't question Lilly's wisdom in not pushing the girls further into a corner. Affecting the breezy air of an old Monty Python rerun, she said, "And now for something completely different . . . how would you like to teach a quilt class at Riverview?"

Lilly looked at her like she'd just proposed a trip to Jupiter.

"Really. To my tea ladies. I talked to them about it. They love the idea." *That's only a slight exaggeration.* "Leda's given her okay. So, it's up to you."

"Jennie, I've got my hands full now."

"With what? What can you actually do about any of this? And they'll pay you. I was thinking of, say, a hundred dollars each. That'd be six hundred."

Lilly didn't respond.

"We could probably make it more."

"No. A hundred dollars is fair. And I can sure use the money."

"It's settled then? You'll do it?"

"Yes."

Chapter Thirteen

The kitchen was spotless.

Lilly gave a final swipe to the sink, then said, "Want to look at some of the fabrics I have on hand? Maybe there's something we can use for the class."

Jennie figured Lilly needed a break from family problems and was glad to go along. "Sounds good," she said, and followed her friend down the hall.

The transplanted island-dweller's room was a soothing change from the heavy Victorian look in the rest of the house. Walls were painted a soft shade between blue and green, so pale it was almost invisible. White sheers let light in. The bed and a low chair were covered in more white, relieved with pillows in blues and greens. The only picture was a watercolor of a beach edged with glistening surf.

Jennie settled into the chair and watched Lilly pull half a dozen pieces of cloth from a closet shelf. "If we use your fabric, we'll reimburse you."

Lilly waved this away.

Jennie started to insist, but was interrupted by the doorbell. She glanced at her watch. Ten after eleven. "That's probably Tom with the kids. Be right back."

Lilly nodded, concentrating on her fabrics.

Jennie was right. It was Tom and the kids. Tommy and Andy bypassed her and darted up the stairs.

Tom glanced at his watch and nodded to Jennie. When the kids had disappeared into the space above, he said, "They shouldn't be here."

"Why?"

"Do you have to ask? There was a double murder here. Obviously it's not the place for a couple of impressionable kids."

She flared back at him. "You make it sound like the building is strewn with corpses."

His only answer was an eloquent shrug.

"Lilly's a good friend. You expect me to abandon her?"

"I didn't say that. But what about your sons? Sometimes I wonder about your priorities."

"What about loyalty? Isn't that a priority? Something worth teaching the kids?"

"Back off, Jen," he said. "This is not a healthy environment for you or the kids."

"Nothing's going on here that's going to hurt them. We're just spending a little time with friends."

He glanced at his watch again. "Look, I have a plane to catch."

"No time to finish what you started?"

"I can't stand here arguing with you."

"The old slash-and-dash. That's admirable."

"Tommy's obsessed with this," was his parting shot. Not that again.

The argument still rankled as she watched Lilly unfurl a piece of fabric.

"It's best to start simple." Lilly's tone was calm, with no hint of the earlier conflict.

Jennie tried to concentrate on her friend's words, but in addition to her own inner turmoil, there was a storm brewing in the adjoining room that couldn't be ignored.

"Butt out! This is none of your business!" Tommy was using his most obnoxious big-brother voice.

Jennie felt like one of those balls fastened to a wooden paddle by a long rubberband—her attention claimed first by Lilly's ideas for the upcoming quilting class, then jerked away by the squabbling kids in the next room.

"This would be a nice background." Lilly ran her fingers over a piece of fabric, emphasizing the flow of swirling lines forming leafy garlands on a subtle tan-on-tan cotton.

From the other room, there was only silence—to a mother, more ominous than the most thunderous crash. "I'd better see if I can settle this," Jennie said, and moved in the direction of Tommy and Andy.

She paused in the doorway to observe the three kids.

Tommy and Charly were huddled on one end of an elaborately-carved Victorian chaise. Tommy's head was bent forward; Charly leaned close, her hand cupped around his ear.

Andy stood alone by the window, his expression a heartbreaking mixture of pain and outrage. He was the first to notice his mother and ran across the room to her. She put her arm around his shoulder and pulled him close, keeping her eyes on the duo on the chaise.

Charly looked up. When she saw Jennie, she immediately pulled away from Tommy.

Tommy glared at his little brother. Whatever the interrupted secret was, he wanted to hear more of it.

"We'll talk at school tomorrow." Charly spoke softly.

"Why can't you talk to me?" Andy demanded.

Tommy said, "'Cause you're a little kid."

Andy responded to his brother's taunt by sprinting across the room and shoving him so hard his head hit the wall behind the chaise.

Jennie separated them before Tommy had a chance to retaliate. "That's enough. We're going home." She turned to Lilly, who had joined them. "I'll call you tomorrow and we'll figure out a schedule for the classes."

"Sure."

Ten minutes later they were in the car, caught in slow-moving Sunday morning traffic.

Jennie glanced up at the rearview mirror, angling her head so she could check each of her sons. Tommy was staring out the window, as far to his side as he could get. Andy leaned against the seatbelt, edging closer to his brother, ready to make peace. As usual, he was willing to endure any indignity to be in Tommy's good graces.

Jennie divided her attention between the traffic and the situation in the back seat, trying to gauge the seriousness of the disagreement. Did this warrant her intervention? Yes, most definitely. Whatever the problem was, it needed to be talked out. No better time than now, when they were all in the car together, relatively free from distractions. A horn sounded. Except for traffic.

"I was disappointed in you guys today." She gave her remark a few seconds to sink in, then went on, "The Wainwright family is going through a bad time. They don't need a lot of garbage from their friends."

"I didn't do anything," Andy said. "Charly and Tommy wouldn't play with me. They just kept whispering."

"So?" Tommy's defense was half-hearted.

Jennie was surprised by his lackluster tone. *Tom's right. He's behaving strangely.*

Andy made a bid for his mother's approval. "It's rude to tell secrets in front of other people. That's what you always say."

Instinct told Jennie that Charly's secret had something to do with the murders and it might be better not to force the issue right now. A one-on-one with Tommy would be better. She said, "You're each a little bit right, a little bit wrong. And I think you both know what you did wrong, so we don't need to beat it to death. Agreed?"

They did. Andy with obvious relief that he wasn't going to be lectured for the physical attack on his brother, Tommy with the same distracted air he'd exhibited since leaving the Wainwright home.

The rest of the ride was quiet, leaving Jennie time to think. She couldn't clear her mind of Charly's outburst, "Mr. Atkinson was a bad man. He deserved to die." What could prompt a nine-year-old child to say that, and to say it with such utter conviction?

* * *

Later after dinner, a Monopoly game, baths, and bedtime, Jennie curled into a corner of the sofa and stared into space, trying to sort out everything that had happened, and most important, how to get Tommy to confide in her.

Soft footsteps padded into the room. Swallowed by an old T-shirt belonging to his father, Tommy looked small and vulnerable. Missing was the confident, know-it-all big brother façade he worked so hard to maintain during the day.

Jennie glanced at the clock. "Can't sleep?"

He shook his head.

She leaned her face up toward his and was rewarded with a minty, toothpaste-flavored kiss. "How about Andy?"

"He's out like a light. Sucking his thumb."

Best to let that pass. "Think a cup of hot chocolate would help?"

"I guess." No enthusiam. A bad sign.

"It would help me. So would a good snuggle."

He joined her on the sofa, curving himself against her.

"What do you say we forget the chocolate and just talk?"

He nodded.

She brushed the fine, straight hair back from his face and kissed his forehead. "Want to tell me what you and Charly were whispering about?"

"We didn't mean to hurt Andy's feelings, but we couldn't tell him. He's a blabbermouth."

"He's only seven."

"I know. That's why we couldn't tell him."

"Can you tell me?"

No answer.

"I get the feeling this is something you need to share."

He twisted so he could look into her eyes. "You won't tell anybody?"

"Not if you don't want me to."

"Promise?"

Something in the nine-year-old's face made her hesitate. She took a deep breath and held it.

Tommy seemed not to notice the hesitation. He blurted out, "Jasmine killed those people."

Jennie let out the breath. She'd been afraid that's what he would say. She tried not to let this show. "Why do you think that?"

"Charly told me."

"Why does she think that? Did she see Jasmine do something?"

"No, but Charly's pretty sure."

"Why? Did she say?"

"No."

"I'm sure she's wrong. Jasmine doesn't even go to Hillcrest. What reason would she have?"

"I don't know. But doesn't it sound like something Jasmine would do?"

"Not really. She acts tough, but she'd never do anything like that."

"You never saw her lose her temper."

Jennie didn't argue. Neither did she agree. No need to tell Tommy she had seen Jasmine lose her temper. Just a couple of days ago. Again, this morning. Against her will, she remembered the threats to herself.

"Please, please, please, God," she prayed silently and

vaguely while she tried to think of a way to reassure Tommy without lying to him.

She had no idea how long they'd been sitting there when she realized Tommy's head had fallen forward and his weight against her side was inert. Having transferred the burden of the terrible secret to his mother, he'd fallen asleep. The problem now belonged to Jennie. What was she to do with it?

Chapter Fourteen

Jennie spread the newspaper on her desk and tried to ignore the Monday morning bustle that pervaded Riverview's hallways. Impossible. A squeaky wheel announced Doreen's presence, but when Jennie looked up, she saw only the back of the wheelchair disappearing into the hall.

Jennie ran to the door and called after her. "Wait!"

Doreen spun halfway around. "I just thought I'd stop in and say hi." She waved toward the paper-strewn desk. "You're busy."

"Nothing important. Don't leave. Are you okay?"

Tears formed in the older woman's eyes and threatened to spill down her cheeks. She guided the chair into the room until she was within touching distance of Jennie.

Jennie reached for her hand. "Of course you're not. You'd have to have ice water in your veins to be okay."

She was rewarded with a tentative smile. "Would it help to talk about it?"

Doreen hesitated and looked again at the desk. "You're in the middle of something."

Jennie scoffed. "Yesterday's paper. It'll wait.

"Articles about the murders?"

"Um-hum. I skimmed them yesterday, wanted to go over them more thoroughly. Have you read them?"

"I have. There was nothing about Ann."

"Do you really think she was murdered?" Jennie held her breath and waited for Doreen's answer.

"The more I think about it, the more sure I am."

I was afraid you'd say that. "Have you told the police?"

"I wanted to talk to you first."

"You want me to call them for you?"

"That would be nice, but it's a bit more complicated than that."

"I don't understand."

Doreen cleared her throat and looked at her hands a moment. "I overheard the argument between you and Jasmine."

"I don't think—"

"Hear me out. I'm not the only one. A lot of people heard. Most of them don't like Jasmine. So far, the police haven't started questioning people here. When they do, and you know they will . . ." Doreen's voice trailed into an expressive silence. She kept her eyes on Jennie's face and let it build.

Jennie repeated the statement she'd made to Tommy.

"Jasmine talks tough, but we both know she's not. She certainly wouldn't murder anyone."

Doreen nodded wisely. "Yes, we know that, but plenty of people don't. They're happy to think the worst of her." Her eyes met Jennie's and it was clear they shared a reluctance to have the police question residents about Jasmine. Doreen continued, "Something else to think about . . . Ann's car was very much like yours. In fact, the only difference was the color."

"That's a pretty obvious difference."

"In the dark it would be easy to mistake one for the other."

"I don't understand. A minute ago you said you didn't think Jasmine would kill anyone. Yet now it sounds like you think she might have."

"It doesn't have to be Jasmine."

"Then who?"

"I don't know." Doreen paused to massage her temples. "I just have this feeling."

"Feeling about what?" Georgia Peterson breezed into the room, clutching a magazine with both hands, oblivious to the fact that the conversation may have been private. When she saw the papers, she went to the desk and squinted down at them. "Been reading about the murders, I see. Good idea." She opened the magazine to reveal a slim notebook concealed between its pages and gave Jennie a sly look. "No use advertising what we're up to."

Jennie didn't comment.

Doreen did. "What on earth are you talking about?"

"Don't try to cut me out of this." Georgie's tone buzzed with waspish energy.

Doreen snapped back at her. "Cut you out of what?"

Jennie knew it was time to intervene. She lay her hand on Georgie's shoulder.

The older woman pulled away, bristling, and waved the notebook at Jennie, ignoring Doreen completely. "This is full of notes, names of people we should question."

Jennie feigned innocence. "Question?"

"Don't pretend you two aren't making plans to investigate the murders. And don't think you can leave me out. I see those newspapers, and I know they're full of stories about Phillip Jeffries and the enemies he's made. I can read, too, you know." She brandished the notebook again. "I listed all the names mentioned and added a few of my own. Those whippersnapper reporters think they know so much, but there's no substitute for living a long time to know what's going on. I've been around more years than any three of them combined, and I've kept my eyes and ears open the whole time." Georgie bounced on her toes the whole time she was making this little speech.

"Mouth too, most of the time." The droll humor in Doreen's voice took some of the sting out of her words.

Whatever Georgie's faults might be, she possessed in spades the ability to laugh at herself. She threw her head back and let out a hearty guffaw, followed by another wave of her notebook. "You'd be making a mistake to leave me out."

Jennie said, "Do you think we have some secret plan to solve the murders? We don't. No one at Riverview is going to play detective." *Except me, of course.*

"So what were you talking about?" Georgie's shrewd eyes narrowed.

Doreen answered the question. "Just chatting."

"Piffle." Georgie turned to Jennie. "Why do you have those papers over there if you aren't interested in the murders?"

"I didn't say I wasn't interested. I said you can't be playing detective. It's too dangerous."

Georgie was not to be put off. "Of course it's dangerous. That's why we have to find whoever did this and stop them." She paused and lowered her already deep voice to add, "Before they strike again. Especially now that we know you're in danger too."

Jennie was quick to ask, "Why do you say I'm in danger?"

A grim smile crept over Georgie's face. "I overheard what Doreen said about Ann's car, and I agree."

Doreen said, "You were eavesdropping?"

Georgie ignored the accusation and held up the notebook. "Don't you even want to see what I've written?"

Jennie glanced at her watch. Not quite eight-thirty. "I have a meeting with Leda in half an hour. Until then . . ." She gathered up the newspapers from her desk and moved them to a nearby table, careful not to disrupt the pages on which she'd circled several articles with heavy black marker. Doreen wheeled herself to the table while Georgia helped Jennie spread the papers out. The three women settled themselves.

"So," Georgia began, "let's see what you have."

"Not much," Jennie said. "I only had time to scan the articles. But I circled everything that had anything to do with the victims. I figured I could read them more carefully before my meeting."

"And we're taking up your time." Doreen's observation was laced with gentle apology.

"Nonsense," Georgia said. "We're helping her." She aimed an intense look toward Jennie. "If you aren't going to play detective, why do you need to know so much about the victims?"

Jennie had no answer for that and knew better than to fake it. She said, "I can't help being curious. The most interesting things aren't from articles, but from letters written to the editor. There's nothing about Atkinson. They all focus on Jeffries. And all were written by people who had personal contact with him during his lifetime." She pointed to another section of newspaper. "The difference between those who admired him and those who didn't is striking." She looked at Georgia's notebook. "So, tell me, what's your take on all this? Was Jeffries really as bad as some make him sound?"

Georgie took a few minutes to scan the letters. "I doubt it. You'll notice the complaints are all from kids he disciplined. Or their parents."

Doreen said, "He was a tough principal, but teachers liked him because he backed them up. At least that's what Ann said." She faltered a little when she said her niece's name, then went on, "I talked to Frances about it too, asked if any of the kids she tutors ever talked about Jeffries."

"What'd she say?"

"She didn't remember anything special, but she's going to keep her ears open."

Jennie's eyes were drawn to an article with a picture of Phillip Jeffries. He was shown presenting an award to the basketball team. Most of the players towered over him by a good six inches. The bodies of the young athletes were exactly what one would expect: lean, gawky, bursting with an energy apparent even in the blurry newsprint. Jeffries, on the other hand, possessed the pear-shaped body of a man who'd spent his life hunched over books. Nevertheless, there was a sense that he was at home in that body, comfortable with what and who he was. His features were regular, though undistinguished except for a mane of snow-white hair, thick and wavy, brushed straight back from a long forehead.

Jennie read aloud from an account written by a former student, now a School Board member: "Phillip Jeffries, a twenty-first-century man for all seasons, had been in this school district in one capacity or another since graduating from college over forty years ago. He planned to retire at the end of the school year, although parents and teachers alike tried to dissuade him from this decision. Now, tragically, we will be deprived of his vast abilities four months sooner than expected. And, even more tragically, Dr. Jeffries will be deprived of the opportunity to enjoy a well-earned rest."

She picked up another section of paper and read, "Phillip Jeffries was a harsh man. He didn't understand the pressures young people face these days. I'm not saying I'm glad he was killed. I'm not, but I'm not surprised either. He hurt a lot of people." She read from another letter, "I'm not one to speak ill of the dead, but I hope when the School Board appoints a new principal, they pick someone with a heart." She looked from

Doreen to Georgie. "Doesn't sound like they're talking about the same person."

Doreen said, "Funny, Tess never says anything about any of this."

Georgie was nodding. "Not a word. Acts like she still works for the government, but I know she's thinking about it."

Jennie said, "Well, that's Tess. She'll speak up when she's ready."

Georgie gave her shoulders an impatient twitch. "Who needs her?"

Doreen ran her fingers over the newspaper picture of Phillip Jeffries, as if to extract the truth from his image. "Not everyone liked him, but I know my niece had a great deal of respect for him."

Georgie waved her notebook. "This is full of names of people who didn't. A lot of people with a motive for murder."

Jennie remembered Elizabeth Wainwright's long-ago conflict with Jeffries. Was her name on that list?

Chapter Fifteen

Jennie left Georgia and Doreen with their heads bent over the notebook and hurried to her 9:00 meeting. Since the quilt class had already been approved and Lilly's plan was well thought out, she wasn't too worried. It was just a matter of scheduling, something most bosses would leave to the activities director, but Leda Barrons wasn't most bosses. She gave new meaning to the term "micromanaging" and Jennie never approached an encounter with her casually. *Be positive,* she reminded herself when she crossed the threshold of the executive director's inner sanctum.

"Good morning, Jennifer." Leda leaned forward and rested her hands on the surface of her desk. "Please sit down." She indicated an excruciatingly uncomfortable chair with a flutter of her pudgy, manicured fingers and continued only after Jennie had complied. "You are extremely well-liked by our residents. Remember, though, no one is indispensable."

"Uh." Jennie stammered momentarily, then anger kicked in. "What does that mean?"

"It has come to my attention that you and your tea ladies plan to solve these murders independent of the police."

"Who told you that?"

"Never underestimate the reach of the grapevine. Do you really think you can do better than the professionals?"

Gossip. "I admit the ladies have their own ideas about this, but I'm not encouraging them."

"Ah, but are you *discouraging* them?"

"I'm doing my best."

"I certainly hope so." Leda removed her small, rimless glasses. "Remember, most of our people are nearing the end of their lives. Our job is to create an atmosphere of tranquility for them."

In Jennie's opinion, the last thing the residents were interested in was tranquility. The majority of them spent their days trying to drum up a little excitement. She kept this to herself and her answer mild. "You can't blame them for being interested. They all know Lilly. Most of them have eaten in her restaurant. It's only natural."

Leda rose to her full, though limited, height, and looked down on Jennie.

Jennie considered standing, an action that would allow her to tower over Leda. She decided against it. Why irritate her further?

Leda said, "Leave it to the police."

Jennie kept her tone conciliatory. "That's what I'm doing."

Leda put the glasses back on and glared at her a few seconds longer before sitting down again. "Have you and Lilly worked out a schedule?"

Without speaking, Jennie handed over the neatly typed list of proposed class times.

"I assume this doesn't conflict with any of our other activities."

"It doesn't."

"Fine." The dismissal was unmistakable. "Remember, your job is to find activities that keep our residents content—not to over-stimulate them."

Jennie left the office, half annoyed, half amused, by the warning.

Leda's long-suffering secretary stopped her on the way out. "I just put a message on your desk."

"Oh? Anything urgent?"

"I don't know. Hope not. Lilly wants you to call."

What's up now? Only one way to find out. Jennie hurried to her office and dialed the number. "Hey, Lilly, it's me. What's up?"

"I need a favor. I have a conference with Jasmine's guidance counselor tomorrow morning, and Elizabeth wants me to go to Phillip Jeffries' funeral with her. She feels she should make an appearance, but she's nervous about facing the widow. It's at ten. Could you possibly go with her? Offer moral support? Just the service. She won't be going to the cemetery or the luncheon."

Jennie shared most people's dislike of funerals, but it didn't occur to her to refuse Lilly. "Sure. I'll drive. Tell her I'll pick her up about nine-thirty."

"Thanks. You've been a rock these past few days. I don't know how I'll ever repay you."

"If in doubt, try chocolate."

"You got it." There was a brief hesitation, then Lilly said, "One more favor?"

"Sure."

"Jasmine still insists she didn't sneak out of the house that night. I believe her."

Jennie didn't comment.

Lilly spoke again. "Could you just keep it to yourself, at least for now?"

"Okay." How could she say no?

After she hung up, she stared into the courtyard, trying to sort her jumbled thoughts. Could she be wrong? Who else would have been up on that porch? And what about Charly's outburst? Why did the child believe her sister had killed the two men? The Memphis papers were full of stories about Jeffries. Why wasn't there more about Atkinson? Did everyone assume he'd simply been in the wrong place at the wrong time? Questions nagged at her, as impossible to ignore as a too-tight shoe. She couldn't stop wondering what Goodley knew about Atkinson. She remembered his responses to her questions on Saturday night. He hadn't actually said he didn't know anything about the man. In fact, he hadn't given her any answers. Only evasions.

She dialed the single digit to the executive director's office and waited for the secretary's response. "Hi, Myrna. Is Leda available?"

"I'll check."

Then Leda's voice: "Yes?"

"Listen, I forgot to mention it, but I'll be out of the building for a while. Maybe the rest of the afternoon. I have to pick up some supplies, things for the quilt class." She crossed her fingers. *It's only a small lie.*

Leda cleared her throat.

Jennie plunged ahead. "I'll also be out tomorrow morning. Lilly asked me to take Elizabeth to Phillip Jeffries' memorial service. I didn't feel I could refuse."

"Really? I'm going to that also. Perhaps we could go together?" Leda was all peaches and cream now, with no hint of the earlier conflict.

"Sure." That settled, Jennie fished her keys out of the humongous tote bag and was on her way to River County to see Goodley.

The receptionist, Ms. Dugan, stuck a finger in the magazine she'd been reading when she saw Jennie. "Hi," she said. "You here to see the lieutenant?"

"Yes."

"Wes," Dugan bellowed over her shoulder. "Somebody here to see you."

All of River County's government offices were housed in the same building, a single cavernous room. Cubicles around the perimeter served as offices for department heads. Support personnel worked at desks in the central area. Most people at these desks looked up in response to Dugan's call. Jennie stood straight and resisted the impulse to fluff her hair.

Goodley's cubicle was in a corner at the rear of the building. He peered out, frowning. When he saw Jennie, the frown disappeared. He came forward and pressed the button to buzz her through the door that separated visitors from staff.

"Hi," he said. "Everything okay?"

Jennie smiled, too conscious of Dugan's presence and the other workers' scrutiny to say much. "Can we talk?"

"Sure." He started back toward his work space, but stopped mid-turn and looked at Dugan. "We have a phone system to announce visitors. You might want to try it sometime."

Dugan flushed and mumbled something Jennie didn't hear, but which she assumed was an apology.

Goodley didn't speak again until he and Jennie reached his cubicle and both had seated themselves. "What's on your mind?"

"I wanted to ask you about Atkinson."

"Who?"

"Leonard Atkinson. You know, he was one of the men poisoned at Lilly's place last week."

He picked up a pencil and rolled it between his hands. "I thought we'd already been over that."

"Actually, we were interrupted before you had a chance to tell me about him."

The pencil snapped. "You don't give up, do you? I don't have anything to tell you about him."

"Does that mean you don't know anything? Or you don't intend to share what you know?"

"What difference does it make? Those crimes weren't committed in my jurisdiction. It's up to the Memphis police to find out who's responsible. I can't interfere. There are procedures to be followed."

"But."

"No buts. It's none of my business. Even less of yours."

"I just want—"

"It doesn't matter what you want. If you came to see

me for something personal, like maybe you like my company." He paused to look at her and when she didn't answer, went on, "That's not why you're here, is it?"

Goodley's face was not one that reflected what was in his mind, at least not to anyone who didn't know him well. Jennie was just beginning to be able to see past the careful mask he maintained, and right now she saw a war of emotions far beyond anything she was prepared to deal with. "I do like your company."

"But that's not why you came."

She shook her head, contrite.

"Then I can't help you."

She stood up and held out her hand. "I understand."

He ignored the proffered hand. "No, I don't think you do." When she didn't answer, he added, "I'll walk you to your car."

They threaded their way through the maze of desks and filing cabinets toward the exit, close together, but not touching. Not a single set of eyes rose to meet theirs. The only sounds were the shuffling of paper and the click of computer keyboards. And Jennie felt more exposed than when people were frankly staring at her.

Chapter Sixteen

After Jennie said good-bye to Goodley, she sat in the parking lot, pondering her next move. Should there be a next move? *Absolutely. I can't give up on this. Nobody even mentions Atkinson. Except Charly. Press doesn't seem interested. The police?* She reached down and turned the key, bringing the engine to life. *Maybe they need a nudge.*

River County Consolidated High School was a little over half a mile from the police station. The building looked spanking new, a single story, spread over the undulating land in modules connected by glass passageways. The parking lot was filled with an assortment of vehicles with dented sides, scratched paint, and taped windows.

Jennie smiled, remembering her first car, a 1980 Chevy Caprice her grandmother had decided to retire. She passed a row of motorcycles, parked in a spot marked VISITOR and headed for the double doors that appeared to be the main entrance to the sprawling complex. Inside, the halls buzzed with a throng of humanity reminiscent of a department store half an hour before closing time on Christmas Eve.

Jennie caught the eye of a youth with a stringbean physique and a shaved head. "Can you tell me where the office is?"

He jerked his thumb over his left shoulder.

A bell rang, and the halls emptied.

Jennie went through the designated door. An affable-looking woman in a flowered tunic and green slacks hummed while she watered plants. Teased, bright blond hair and rouged cheeks made her look like an extension of her clothing, her head the topmost blossom in a psychedelic bouquet. "Can I help you?" You could almost smell honeysuckle when she spoke.

"I'd like to see the principal." Jennie wished she'd thought to look up the name.

"Do you have an appointment?"

"No."

"Maybe I can help. I'm Bertie Lennox, Mrs. Wyandotte's assistant."

"I really need to speak with the principal."

"You should've called ahead. She has a full schedule." The woman's manner was friendly, but no-nonsense.

Jennie reconsidered her first impression. Better cut to the chase. "It's about Leonard Atkinson."

There was a narrowing of eyes and an intake of breath, so slight Jennie wondered if she'd imagined them. "Wait here."

Time stretched. The clock over the cluttered desk

ticked. Hints of a whispered exchange filtered through the closed door. *She's not going to see me. Not willingly.* Jennie crossed the outer office, paused at the threshold, gulped down a dozen years of intimidation, and entered the room without knocking.

"Excuse me." Horror and disbelief merged theatrically in Ms. Lennox's protest.

Jennie ignored her and went directly to the fifty-something woman behind the desk. She extended her hand. "I'm Jennifer Connors. I'd like to speak with you about one of your former teachers, Leonard Atkinson."

The dignified woman rose, but ignored Jennie's outstretched hand. "I'm Sylvia Wyandotte. I don't discuss my teachers with outsiders." She spoke firmly, as though addressing a wayward student.

The assistant, hands on hips, placed herself between Jennie and Wyandotte.

Jennie spoke to the principal over Lennox's shoulder. "Just a few minutes. That's all I'm asking."

The two women looked at her with unchanging stony faces.

Jennie lifted her chin. *This is for Lilly.* She said, "I'm a friend of the owner of the restaurant where Mr. Atkinson died."

Sylvia Wyandotte hesitated, then said, "I'll handle it, Bertie." She nodded to the outer office.

Ms. Lennox left, closing the door behind her, skewering Jennie with a poisoned look on her way out.

Mrs. Wyandotte indicated a chair opposite the desk. "Remember, you promised this would be brief."

"I'll get right to the point. Why did Mr. Atkinson leave here?"

The principal's smile looked pasted on. "I'm afraid that's confidential."

Jennie ploughed ahead. "He left in the middle of the year, right after Christmas. Why?"

The smile became brighter, more artificial. "I suppose I can tell you that much. A math teacher at a school in Memphis had a stroke and the position became available. Unfortunately, a rural school district like ours can't compete with the more affluent ones."

"The paper said he came highly recommended. In other words, you gave him a good reference." Jennie watched Wyandotte's composure begin to slip and went on, "He must have signed a contract. Did you release him from it?"

A curt nod was the only answer.

"Couldn't you make him honor his commitment?"

"I didn't want to stand in his way." Wyandotte rose from her chair. "I've answered your questions. I have a number of things to do this afternoon."

The woman's manner convinced Jennie that her instincts were right. Something about Atkinson was being hidden and she was determined to find out what it was. How? One thing usually scared people with something to hide. "Would you rather talk to the press?"

"I've given them a statement."

"I know. I read it."

"Everything I said is true."

"What about the things you didn't say?"

Wyandotte didn't respond.

The two women sized each other up—Wyandotte

standing behind her desk, Jennie firmly rooted in the chair.

Jennie broke the silence. "Are you familiar with Jill Newton, the TV reporter? She's interested in this. I could call her. See if she can figure out what happened." With that, she rose and started toward the door.

"Wait."

Jennie returned to the chair.

Wyandotte sat down. She opened her mouth, closed it, bit her lip. She swiveled her chair toward the wall.

Jennie sat tight.

The chair rotated back, and Wyandotte faced Jennie again. "I think I always knew this day would come." She paused, arranged the items on her desk into an orderly queue. When she looked up, her features were as carefully composed as the queue. "What I say is to be held in confidence. Promise me that."

"I can't promise. Two people are dead."

"I'm aware of that. But they're beyond hurt. We have to consider the living."

Who's she protecting? "You know something about Atkinson. That's obvious. Maybe it led to his death. You can't keep it a secret."

Wyandotte shuffled a cup holding pencils around a clear plastic container of paperclips.

Jennie watched, her patience fraying. "The restaurant where the murders were committed belongs to a friend of mine, a good friend. She's got three kids and no way to support them. Until this is cleared up, her life's on hold. When you're considering the living, maybe you should think about them." She made no attempt to hide her anger.

Wyandotte squared her shoulders as though she'd made a decision. "What do you want to know?"

"Why did Atkinson leave?"

Seconds passed. Ms. Lennox could be heard moving about on the other side of the door. Finally, the principal answered, "I admit there was a problem, but he promised—"

"What was the problem?"

"He, uh, it involved cheating. Athletics."

"He encouraged kids to cheat?"

There was an affirmative nod. Wyandotte's pinched expression said there was more.

Jennie took a few seconds to process this. "Were drugs involved?"

Another nod.

"Illegal drugs? Steroids?"

"Yes." She expelled a long breath, looked relieved.

"Did you notify the authorities? Parents?"

Wyandotte held up her hand, palm out. "Let me explain." She paused, closed her eyes, apparently gathering her thoughts, then continued, "Leonard Atkinson was a charismatic man, charming, the sort of teacher young people gravitate to. He joined our faculty a year ago last fall and was immediately popular with the students." She took another long breath. "There was a lot going on at the time. Exciting things." She spread her hands, indicating their surroundings. "We had this new building, a modern athletic field for the first time, but no money to pay a coach. Len volunteered to organize a football team, said he'd do it without extra compensation."

"Didn't that bother you? Raise a red flag?"

"In hindsight, yes. At the time . . ." Wyandotte

looked up to meet Jennie's gaze. "It came about naturally. He spent time, a lot of time, with difficult students, the ones we call 'at risk.' He suggested the team as a way of getting some of them involved." She looked away from Jennie, dug out a handful of paperclips and strung them into a chain before she continued, "Our kids did well. They were beating teams from schools with long-established programs. They were proud. We all were. It took me a while to realize they were doing too well."

"How'd you figure it out?"

"A chance remark actually. It was a Saturday. Right after a game. Our kids had won. I jokingly asked Leonard if he was feeding his players a magic formula. He laughed, just as I expected him to, but his wife . . . have you met Mrs. Atkinson?"

Jennie remembered the scared rabbit who'd visited Riverview with Ann Tull just before the accident. "Briefly. Her name's Martha, right?"

Mrs. Wyandotte nodded. "Anyway, she was standing beside him and her reaction . . . I can't tell you exactly why, but I knew something was wrong. I didn't pursue it at the time, but it bothered me all weekend. I called Leonard into my office on Monday and confronted him."

"He admitted it?"

"Not at first, but when I kept after him, he did."

Jennie asked, "What did you do then?"

"I called parents immediately. There were five students involved. They all pleaded with me not to go to the authorities."

"That makes no sense at all! Don't they know how dangerous steroids are?"

Wyandotte leaned back in her chair and looked at Jennie. "Keep in mind this a rural community, not wealthy. No one wanted a scandal where their sons were concerned. Some were probably hoping for scholarships."

"Didn't you feel a responsibility to the other kids? Other districts?"

Wyandotte thrust her chin forward. "Leonard assured me, all of us, two of the parents are members of our School Board, he would never do anything like this again."

"And you believed him?"

"After the initial meeting, I turned the matter over to the School Board."

"What did they do?"

"Atkinson was dismissed, of course."

"But you recommended him for the position in Memphis."

Wyandotte sat rigidly erect, motionless except for her hands, which picked at the paperclip chain. "I was presented a letter of recommendation and instructed to sign. I did as I was told." Her shoulders sagged.

Against her will, Jennie felt a tug of sympathy that must have shown on her face.

Wyandotte jumped on it. "I've worked hard to become a principal. I'm not a young woman. My retirement is—" She stopped abruptly, her eyes pleading her cause.

Jennie refused to be deflected. "Who gave you the letter to sign?"

"I'm afraid I can't tell you that."

"Afraid? Why?"

"I've said all I intend to." Her eyes had become flint hard.

She means it. "It doesn't matter if you tell me or not. But you have to call the police and tell them. It might change the investigation. Of the two murders in Memphis, I mean."

Wyandotte made a tent of her hands and studied her fingertips. After a few seconds, she looked at Jennie and said, "Leonard's widow is, uh, fragile. The publicity . . ."

Another domino ready to topple. Sad. But Jennie wondered what she could do. *Something.* "If it'll make you feel better, I'll go see her and warn her. I know you have to keep a distance, so I'll do it."

"Thank you. Martha's a good person and, right now, very alone. She doesn't deserve to be hurt any more."

"I understand what you're saying. I don't want to hurt her either, but you can't keep this information to yourself."

Wyandotte attempted a smile. "I don't suppose you know the number of the Memphis police?"

"Why don't you start with the River County police? I know that number. Ask to speak to Lieutenant Weston Goodley. He'll tell you where to go from there." Jennie wrote down the number and watched the other woman punch it in.

Chapter Seventeen

Following Sylvia Wyandotte's directions, Jennie turned onto Sugar Bottom Road and headed north. For the first three miles, the gravel lanes lay ruler-straight with flat, dormant fields on either side. Ahead, the road seemed to dead-end in a forest.

I must be getting close. She checked the rearview mirror and, when she saw no cars approaching, pulled over and stopped to study the precisely-drawn map lying in the seat. It showed a sharp bend to the right just before the wooded area, leaving an expanse between the road and the trees. ATKINSON was printed in neat block letters next to an *X* just beyond the curve. After that, Wyandotte had drawn a larger *X* and had written: "If you pass a big house with columns and white fences, you've gone too far."

Jennie looked up from the map to verify her position. Two deer emerged from a break in the trees. They stopped to peer in her direction before they bounded across the fields, seemingly unfettered by gravity. She watched, spellbound by their grace, until they disappeared. She then guided the car back into the road and drove on until she came to a driveway.

Stick-on squares with curling edges spelled out A K NSON on a plain tin mailbox. Jennie pulled in behind an older model Subaru and a sporty little red Camry with a handlettered FOR SALE sign in the back window. She took a few seconds to study the two-story farmhouse, a no-nonsense rectangle with peeling paint that had once been white. There were gaps in the gingerbread trim on the porch. A chain link fence separated the yard from the fields around it. A sign, BEWARE OF DOG, was fastened to the gate.

Jennie stepped out of the car. Mindful of the warning, she looked around before opening the gate. A muffled yipping came from inside the house. *Doesn't sound too ferocious.* She made her way up the porch steps and knocked. The yipping became frantic. The door opened a crack, and Martha peered out.

"Hi, I'm Jennie Connors. We met the other day at Riverview."

Martha bent to pick up the dog, a mixed breed that looked predominantly terrier. "Shush, you'll scare the lady," she cooed into its ear. When the dog calmed, she opened the door further. "Come on in. I remember who you are. Don't mind Fancy. She wouldn't hurt a flea."

Jennie entered and reached out a tentative hand to stroke Fancy's head. "What about the sign on the gate?"

"Oh, that was my husband's idea. He thought it would keep prowlers away."

The two of them stood looking at each other. Jennie read apprehension in Martha's eyes. *She can probably guess why I'm here.*

Martha spoke first. "Would you like to sit down?"

"Sure." She followed Martha into a room just off the entryway.

Piles of clothing covered the sofa and boxes took up most of the floor space.

"Over here." Martha set the dog down and threaded her way between boxes to two chairs wedged in the corner.

Jennie stepped around a carton of books and seated herself. Sitting didn't diffuse the tension. She knew the longer she waited, the harder it would be to speak. A deep breath gave her courage. "I just left Mrs. Wyandotte."

Martha sat rigid, perched on the edge of her chair.

"I know about your husband. Why he left the school here, I mean."

She gripped the arms of the chair, whitening her knuckles, but did not speak.

"I came to warn you . . . there's going to be publicity. She has to call the police. Tell them—"

"Why? It's over now. He can't do it any more."

"It isn't over until whoever killed him and Phillip Jeffries is in jail."

Tears began to seep from Martha's eyes. She made no effort to wipe them away.

Jennie wanted to cry herself. *I had to do it.* Aloud, she said, "The authorities would have found out sooner or later. This may help them solve the crimes. Then you can start putting the whole thing behind you."

"Maybe it had nothing to do with Leonard. The papers say Dr. Jeffries had a lot of enemies." She stared out the window, never once looking at Jennie, though they were so close their knees almost touched.

"Yes," Jennie conceded. "Maybe the poison was intended only for Dr. Jeffries. It's possible your husband was just in the wrong place at the wrong time." She willed the other woman to make eye contact. "I know how hard this must be for you."

"No. You don't." She spoke without emotion, still ignoring the tears. "No one can even begin to imagine how I ashamed I am."

"Ashamed? You didn't do anything."

"I tried. I pleaded with him. Every time it happened—"

"This happened before?"

There was a long pause, then a nod.

Jennie leaned forward, encouraging Martha to add more.

Martha took a rough swipe at the tears and said, "It started with Len himself, back in high school." A long shudder forced her to stop and catch her breath.

Jennie prompted her to go on. "Is that where you met?"

"Yes. We grew up together. A little town in east Texas. Len wanted to play football. He wasn't really big enough, but . . . where we lived, you weren't a man if you didn't play football. So he got himself some steroids."

"From the coach?"

Martha shook her head. "Our coach didn't allow that sort of thing. Some did, but ours didn't. Anyway, Len and one of his buddies went down to Mexico. They started bulking up real fast, and the coach figured it out.

He kicked them both off the team. After that, Len never took the stuff himself, but he knew where to get it."

When she didn't add more, Jennie asked, "He supplied other athletes?"

Martha nodded. "All through college and then after, in his teaching jobs. We've been married twenty years and lived in fourteen different places."

Jennie asked, "But why? If he kept getting caught?"

"He never gave up the dream of being a football hero. If he couldn't be a player, he wanted to be a coach. I tried to reason with him, but he said everybody did it. He just thought he had bad luck. 'One championship team. That's all I need.' That's what he kept saying. He was always calling me in to look at some player on TV. 'Look at him,' he'd say. 'You think he's not on something?' "

Martha finally broke down. She buried her face in her hands. Her body shook with sobs. Fancy raced across the room and jumped into her lap, alternately growling at Jennie and licking her mistress's face.

Jennie moved to the arm of the other chair, sat on it, and started to put her arm around the distraught woman's shoulder.

Fancy bared tiny, needlelike teeth.

Jennie pulled back her hand, uncertain what to do next. *Give her a little space.* "Maybe I could make us both a cup of tea. Would that be okay?"

A mumbled "Yes," broke through the sobs.

Jennie found the kitchen with no trouble. A kettle rested on the stove. A canister marked TEA sat nearby. She looked around while she waited for the water to boil. In contrast to the clutter of the living room, the kitchen was tidy and immaculate. On the window sill was a small statue of a man in a flowing robe with a carpenter's square in one hand, a staff in the other. Jennie recognized St. Jude, patron saint of lost causes. *She must have prayed to him a lot.* Through the window she could see a field stretching on both sides and, beyond that, the woods. Motion stirred in her peripheral vision. She leaned forward and looked to the right. Half a dozen horses frolicked near a tall structure. Jennie looked closer and saw that the building was a barn, brilliantly white, trimmed with dark planks placed vertically at the corners and outlining the door and loft window.

By the time Jennie returned to the living room, Martha had composed herself and was burrowed deep in the chair. Fancy lay curled in her lap, alert, her eyes on Jennie.

"I'm sorry," Martha said, dabbing at her eyes with a tissue. "I usually have more control."

"Nothing to be sorry for. Cry as much as you need to."

She shrugged. "I've learned it doesn't do much good." She reached for one of the cups Jennie had set on a nearby table.

Glad for the emotional respite, Jennie looked around and realized what she had thought of as clutter was actually an organized assortment of clothes: a stack of folded khakis, a pile of men's undershirts, socks rolled into neat bundles.

As though reading her thoughts, Martha said, "I'm going through Len's things, deciding what to throw away, what to give to someone."

Already?

Martha answered the unasked question. "I'm not sure how long I'll be staying here. We've been renting this place from Constance Barlow. Without Len's salary . . ." There was no need to finish the sentence. She lifted her chin and smiled at Jennie. "I don't suppose you know anyone who needs a secretary? Maybe the place where you work?"

"I'll ask our director, but I'm pretty sure the answer will be no." The forlorn look on Martha's face made her add, "Maybe she'll know someone who does."

Martha nodded and lifted her chin, but the effort to hold back tears was evident.

"Other than a job, is there anything I can do? If you need a friend, someone to talk to, I'm just a phone call away." Knowing her insistence that Mrs. Wyandotte call the police was partly the cause of Martha's pain, Jennie couldn't help wondering how welcome her offer would be. Still, if they'd moved so often, she doubted Martha could have many close friends. And the death of a spouse, even one such as Atkinson, was not something to face alone. There'd been no mention of a funeral. Dare she ask? *Yes.* "Will there be, uh, a memorial service?"

"No. After the autopsy, he'll be cremated. I don't feel up to a service. Especially now that everybody will know what he did." She lifted her chin again, the picture of defiance.

No ceremony of any kind? Jennie was taken aback. To break the long silence, she asked, "Do you have family around?"

"No. My family's all in Texas."

"Won't they—"

"They wrote Len off long ago. Me too, when I wouldn't leave him."

"His family?"

Martha shook her head, offered no explanation.

"Don't hide too long. The longer you wait, the harder it'll be to face people."

Martha surprised Jennie by agreeing. "I've thought of that. I should go to Phillip Jeffries' service tomorrow. I don't suppose . . ." She let her voice drift.

There was no doubt in Jennie's mind what she intended to say. "I'm going to the service. I already have two passengers, but you're welcome to come with us. The other people are Elizabeth Wainwright, she's—"

"I read in the paper about her old run-in with Dr. Jeffries. She's probably almost as nervous as I am."

"Believe me, she is. The other person is my boss, Leda Barrons. I don't know what her connection to Jeffries is, but she probably has one. She's from an old Memphis family, knows everybody who's anybody."

"Oh,"—a long pause—"will she mind my being with you?"

"Of course not." Jennie was quick to reassure Martha, but had no idea if her words were true.

Jennie stopped for lunch at a roadside diner where she was sure she wouldn't run into anyone she knew. She slipped into a corner booth and declined a menu. "I'll have a cheeseburger and fries." *Fat, cholesterol and carbs in one handy-dandy shot. Just what I need.* While she waited for her food, Jennie thought over what she'd learned about Leonard Atkinson.

Did any of it tie in to Lilly's girls? Did it explain why

Jasmine would sneak out at night? Jennie didn't see how. She wouldn't be getting steroids from him. Other illegal drugs? It still didn't add up. Jasmine was in senior high, not the junior high school where Atkinson taught. On the other hand, steroids might account for her violent outbreaks and moodiness. Not necessarily, though. Lilly says Jasmine was born in a bad mood. Jennie was convinced Atkinson's shady history was involved, but still hadn't worked out the connection.

She thought back to the night of the murders. That was the first time she'd seen Martha Atkinson, screaming like a banshee and trying to climb into the ambulance that carried her husband away. *Was that before or after I saw someone on the balcony?* Jennie closed her eyes and tried to fix the sequence in her mind.

A nasal voice and the thud of a thick plate landing on the formica tabletop broke her concentration. "You need ketchup?"

"Yes, please," Jennie answered and vowed to put the murders out of her mind, at least for a while. She was nibbling a french fry when it hit her. *Martha was at the restaurant that night. What did she eat?*

When she got home, she checked the answering machine and found messages from Goodley, Tom, and Leda. All three said it was important.

Tom's message probably concerned the kids, so he got priority. Nothing new there. He just wanted to know if Tommy was still obsessing over the murders. She calmed him down, but didn't tell him their son had confided to her that Charly believed her sister had killed two people. No sense adding fuel to the fire in his belly.

She was pretty sure she knew what Goodley wanted, so she called Riverview next and asked to speak to Leda.

Leda wasted no time on pleasantries. "Georgia Peterson wants to go Phillip Jeffries' service tomorrow. I told her I'm going with you and that I was sure you wouldn't mind her riding along."

"Uh, space is a problem. I already told you Elizabeth would be going with us and today I invited Martha Atkinson."

"Who's Martha Atkinson?"

"The widow of Leonard Atkinson, the other victim. Anyway, if Georgie comes, that'll make five. My little Bug can't handle more than four." She waited for Leda to offer to drive and take Georgie with her. No such luck.

"We'll take the van. That will be better anyway. It's much more comfortable."

Jennie didn't argue. "Fine. I'll see you at nine-thirty."

That left Goodley. As expected, he wanted to know if Jennie had prompted the telephone call he'd received from Sylvia Wyandotte.

"Sort of." There was a long pause. Jennie resisted the temptation to fill the dead air space.

Goodley finally said, "Why didn't you tell me about Atkinson yourself?"

"I didn't know when I talked to you."

"When did you find out? And how?"

"I knew there was something a little off. So, when you wouldn't listen to me, I went to the school and asked a few questions."

All she heard from the other end was a long sigh.

"Isn't it a good thing I did?"

"Not necessarily."

"It isn't important?"

"I didn't say that. It's important, but the police would have found out. You shouldn't be involved. There are procedures to be followed."

Procedures again. It's amazing anything ever gets done. She changed the subject. "Did you call the Memphis police?"

"I did, not that it's any of your business."

I guess I deserved that. Deserved or not, she didn't want to end on a sour note. "So, you're involved in the investigation after all?"

"Not the murders. They were committed in Memphis, not River County. We're separate entities. I'll talk to parents up here about the alleged steroid use. If I learn anything that might relate to the murders, I'll share it with the investigating officer in Memphis. And I'm going to Dr. Jeffries' funeral tomorrow."

"But it's not in your jurisdiction."

"So, I'll be a little over the line. An unofficial visit."

Never thought I'd hear him say that. "I'll see you there."

"You're not doing more investigating?" The words came out like whiplash.

"No. I'm driving Riverview's van because one of our residents wants to go. Plus, I have some other passengers." Wouldn't he love to know that the resident in question was convinced she could do a better job of solving the crime than the police? And wouldn't he be surprised to see that Atkinson's widow was one of the other passengers? She said good-bye and hung up, anticipating the next day with mixed feelings. Funerals were never fun. This one, at least, would not be dull.

Chapter Eighteen

Jennie hustled the boys onto the school bus and hurried back to the house to check the morning paper before changing for the funeral.

She put the kettle on and, while she waited for it to whistle, scanned the front page for news about Atkinson's shady past. Nothing there. Obviously the Memphis police hadn't shared their information with the press yet. She turned to the page where they published letters to the editor. Most of that section was taken up by responses to news stories about the murders. The letterwriters ignored Atkinson and concentrated on Hillcrest's late principal, Phillip Jeffries, the man whose memorial service Jennie would be attending later this morning. And again, the letters were evenly divided between those who believed Jeffries had gotten what he deserved and those who thought he was a latter-day saint.

She left the house a few minutes after nine and

pulled into Riverview's parking lot at nine-twenty. She was surprised to see handyman Martin Willis seated behind the wheel of the van. Maybe Leda had reconsidered and asked him to drive the Riverview people. Before this thought had time to take flight, Martin rolled down the window and yelled, "Got her all gassed up for you."

"Thanks," Jennie said, and mentally added, *for small favors.* Not that she minded driving the van. She'd taken a class qualifying herself to operate the bulky vehicle and frequently used it to transport residents on outings. But today she'd have preferred her little Bug, with only Elizabeth and Martha as passengers.

She parked her car, accepted the van keys from Martin, and looked toward Riverview's exit ramp, where Georgie Peterson, Frances Lavery, Faye Dodd, Tess Zumwalt, and Vera Sanborn were assembled. All were dressed in their Sunday best. All looked deceptively guileless. Jennie sent up a quick prayer: "Just get me through this."

Leda Barrons was nearby, frowning at her watch. She glanced up, saw Jennie, and came striding forward. Outfitted in her own unique blend of society matron and dress-for-success, Leda looked anything but guileless. The simple black suit was beautifully cut, the fabric obviously expensive, but nothing could disguise the barrel shape of its wearer. Still, Jennie had to admit, Riverview's executive director possessed that elusive quality referred to as presence.

"We have some additional passengers. Your tea ladies decided to come. All of them. Except Doreen, of course, poor dear." Leda did not sound happy.

Before Jennie had time to comment, a dark green

Subaru pulled into the space near where she and Leda were standing.

Jennie greeted its occupant and introduced her to Leda. "This is Martha Atkinson." To Martha she said, "We have a few more passengers, so we're taking the van."

Martha took a step back from Leda's direct gaze. "I hope you don't mind my tagging along."

Leda had no time to answer before the tea ladies swarmed. They surrounded Martha, buzzing with good will and inquisitiveness.

Jennie wondered what their attitude would be when they heard the news about Martha's late husband. Even a hint of anything to do with illegal substances usually sent them into orbit. She added Martha's name to her prayer.

The appearance of Elizabeth Wainwright crossing the alley from the restaurant diverted Jennie's attention. Elizabeth checked out the crowd assembling near the van and shot a questioning look Jennie's way.

Jennie explained, "Some of our residents wanted to go so we're taking the van."

Elizabeth, gracious as always, smiled.

"We may as well get started." Leda opened the vehicle's front door and seated herself in position to ride shotgun.

Georgie supervised placement of the other passengers, putting herself in the back, with Martha next to her.

Jennie settled into the driver's seat and sent up another prayer.

"Slow down. That light looks ready to change." Leda's voice carried absolute authority.

How does she know? Does she have some kind of zen kinship with traffic lights? Jennie kept her thoughts to herself and glanced at the mirror toward Martha. *Maybe the storm won't break until I get her home.* Too much to expect? Probably.

Leda continued to point out speed limit signs and traffic lights, as well as offering comments on other drivers who looked like they might pose a threat.

Jennie nodded, alternatively smiled and frowned, and basically ignored the unsolicited advice. She turned when a sign announced Charles Street. According to Leda, who was a walking encyclopedia on the history and geography of Memphis, they were half a block from their destination.

The Church of the Little Flower, in stark contrast to its name, was an imposing stone edifice with an arched front door that dwarfed anyone passing through its portal. The church loomed over the surrounding neighborhood, as if daring any challenge to its authority. A few people chatted on the walk in front, but most hurried inside, their collars turned up against the damp wind.

Jennie slowed, looking for a parking place.

"Go to the end of the block and turn right," Leda commanded. "There's a parking lot in back and a ramp leading to the rear entrance.

Jennie followed the directive and parked in a spot near the ramp.

The interior of the church was as forbidding as its exterior. Tall, leaded-glass windows admitted scant light. Ornate chandeliers, suspended from chains, cast shadows, but did nothing to relieve the gloom.

Leda marched down the center aisle, with the five tea ladies following in a cluster. Jennie, Elizabeth, and Martha brought up the rear. Leda chose a pew near the front and stopped to let the others enter before she took the aisle seat.

Jennie's elbow touched Martha's as they stepped sideways into the pew. The other woman jumped as though she'd been struck. Jennie whispered, "Sorry," and glanced over at her.

Unshed tears glistened in Martha's eyes.

Jennie lay a hand on her arm. "You okay?"

Martha bobbed her head, though she looked anything but okay. Dark circles underscored her eyes, and her lips were compressed into a tight, straight line.

Jennie doubted she could make it through the service. She put her hand on Martha's arm and said, "This is too much for you right now."

"Shh." Leda's reptilian hiss traveled down the pew. The ladies' heads swiveled from Leda to Jennie, spectators ready for either tragedy or farce. Elizabeth was harder to read. She concentrated on a spot near the altar and picked at her cameo brooch with restless fingers.

Jennie ignored them all and whispered to Martha, "We don't have to stay." She wasn't sure if Martha heard her.

The congregation rose for the first hymn.

Martha reached for a hymnal. The book slipped from her hand and struck the pew in front of them before landing on the floor with a sharp crack. Martha sat down, but made no attempt to retrieve the hymnal.

Jennie picked it up and replaced it in the rack. She scribbled a note in the margin of her bulletin: "We'll wait in the van," and handed the bulletin to Elizabeth, who passed it along to Leda.

Leda read the note, looked over and made a shooing

motion with both hands, then, at least outwardly, devoted full attention to the hymn, "Holy Ghost, Dispel Our Sadness."

Jennie placed an arm around Martha's thin shoulders and guided her out of the pew to the side aisle. There was no unobtrusive path to the back door and the parking lot so they exited the church by the front. Outside, a biting wind whipped their coats around their legs as they made their way to the parking lot.

A *tap, tap* of stiletto-heeled footsteps on the concrete walk kept pace behind them.

Jennie turned when they reached the van and recognized the TV reporter, Jill Newton, whose button-bright eyes told her that Leonard Atkinson's history was now common knowledge. She pushed the control that unlocked the van, pulled the door open, and shoved Martha inside.

The reporter caught up just as Jennie closed the door. "Mrs. Connors."

"Yes?"

"Is the service over?"

"No." Jennie glanced at the van. The windows, tinted dark to keep out sun glare, exposed Martha's outline, but not sufficient detail to reveal her identity.

"You left early. Why?"

"Someone in our party wasn't feeling well, so I came out here with her to wait for the others."

"Who's in your party?"

"Some of the ladies from Riverview wanted to attend the funeral." It wasn't a lie. And Jennie certainly felt no compulsion to tell the whole truth to the TV reporter.

Newton asked, "Do you know if Mrs. Atkinson is in there?" She nodded toward the church.

"Mrs. Atkinson?"

"Leonard Atkinson, the other victim. His widow. Do you know her?"

"I've met her."

"Did you see her in the church?"

Jennie hesitated. "I don't think she's in there." Again, not a lie, but Jennie crossed her fingers behind her back.

Newton seemed to accept this and changed direction. "I understand Ann Tull, Dr. Jeffries' replacement, was related to a resident of Riverview."

"Yes." Jennie didn't want to arouse Newton's suspicions by refusing to talk to her, so she played it safe and answered the questions, but kept her answers short.

"And she was killed in an accident." The reporter's pause left room for Jennie to comment. When she didn't, Newton persisted, "Doesn't that seem like a lot of bad luck in a short time for one school?"

Jennie didn't answer this either.

Newton wouldn't give up. "I understand there's some question about the accident. Do you know anything about that?"

"No."

Newton looked toward the walk leading to the front of the church, then toward the edge of the parking lot, where the TV van was parked. "Any idea how much longer it's going to be?"

Jennie shook her head. "Hard to tell. Services vary."

The reporter waved to someone in the TV van. A

burly man with a camcorder emerged. As though by signal, both started walking around the church toward the front.

Jennie saw Goodley's gray Jetta parked a few spaces from the TV van. She started to wave, but conscious of the reporter's presence, put her hand in her pocket. No need to alert Ms. Newton of any connection between her and the police lieutenant. She wondered how long he'd been there and if he'd seen her with Martha Atkinson. If so, would he recognize Martha as Atkinson's widow? Suddenly aware of the cold wind, Jennie got into Riverview's van herself.

Martha was huddled in the back, her eyes closed.

"You okay?" Jennie asked.

Martha answered without opening her eyes. "I'm fine, just resting."

They waited, each lost in her own thoughts, until people began to exit the church. Jennie watched for her ladies, and when they appeared, went to meet them.

They came out the rear door. Georgie was first down the ramp, with Frances, Faye, Tess, and Vera in her wake. Elizabeth and Leda were a couple of steps behind them. While Jennie watched, a tall, distinguished-looking woman came hurrying up and placed her hand on Elizabeth's shoulder. Constance Barlow. Again. Jennie watched the two women step to the side, Barlow talking, Elizabeth listening, while other people filed past them. *She wants to buy the Wainwright place. Elizabeth is trying to talk Lilly into accepting her offer.* Jennie was incensed the Barlow woman would use a funeral as an opportunity to talk to Elizabeth without Lilly present.

She crossed the parking lot and met them.

Georgie asked, "What happened?"

"Martha wasn't feeling well."

"I could see that for myself. I want to know what happened."

"Nothing. We just came out here in the fresh air. She's waiting in the van now." Jennie pushed the button to unlock the doors. "Why don't you join her? I'll be there in a minute."

The tea ladies made a beeline to the van.

Poor Martha. Jennie had a guilty flash. It didn't last long. *She'll have to fend for herself. I need to get Elizabeth away from Barlow.* She was surprised when Barlow detached herself from Elizabeth and came gliding forward.

The other woman extended a gloved hand. "I'm Constance Barlow." Her accent was unmistakably Old South, her smile dazzling.

Jennie accepted the proffered hand. "I'm—"

"No need to introduce yourself. You're Jennie Connors. I've heard all about you and your good work with the people at Riverview."

Jennie didn't know quite how to respond to that.

Leda saved her. "Yes, we at Riverview are quite proud of Jennifer."

You are?

Elizabeth spoke up for the first time. "Jennie, Constance has invited us to lunch tomorrow at her farm."

Jennie's confusion must have shown in her face because Barlow rushed to explain. "I was telling Elizabeth I remember visiting her home with my mother when I was a little girl. I came across some old photos I think she'd enjoy. I have other pictures too, some you might be interested in. There are people I don't recognize. They may be younger versions of some of your Riverview people."

"I'd love to see them, but I have to work tomorrow."

Leda piped up again. "I'm sure we can find someone to fill in. It's a good idea for you to look through the pictures. You might find a little piece of one of our resident's past. That sort of thing always delights them."

Jennie started to protest.

Leda said, "I insist."

So it was settled. Jennie was going to lunch at the home of land baroness Constance Barlow tomorrow. She had no clue why she'd really been invited. And no doubt it would prove an interesting experience.

Chapter Nineteen

The trip back to Riverview was quiet. Martha remained huddled in her corner of the backseat with her eyes closed. The tea ladies, even Georgie, left her alone. Elizabeth gazed, sphinxlike, out the window. Leda clasped and unclasped the purse in her lap, too preoccupied to monitor the traffic situation.

Jennie was left to her own reflections. *Why does she want me to have lunch with Barlow? Is it really just the pictures?* She glanced sideways at her boss. Somehow that seemed too straightforward for Leda. Advice from her ever-practical mother came to mind: "If you want a question answered, ask it." Jennie cleared her throat. "Leda, why do you want me to have lunch with Constance Barlow?"

Leda jolted to attention. "I thought I made that clear. You might find a photograph of one of our residents when they were young. You know how they love that sort of thing."

155

"I had a feeling there was more to it."

Leda faced Jennie and whispered, "I'm surprised you can't see it."

Jennie whispered back, "See what?"

Leda directed a quick glance back to where Elizabeth sat. After a short hesitation, she removed a small notebook and scribbled on one of its pages. She placed the notebook on her purse and turned it so Jennie could read the words: "The Barlow charities," with "charities" underlined three times.

Ah hah. She wants some of the Barlow money for Riverview. Always thinking, our Leda. Well, since my salary is paid out of that money, I guess I shouldn't turn up my nose.

Quiet returned to the vehicle. Too quiet for Leda, apparently. She reached over and switched on the radio, tuned, as usual, to an oldies station. They were playing a slow, dreamy piece, vaguely familiar to Jennie, obviously better known to her elderly passengers. Georgie started to hum along and was joined by the other tea ladies. Elizabeth continued to stare out the window, but her stoic expression softened. Only Martha showed no reaction. The song ended. A perky voice announced that the news was coming right up.

Geez. No. Jennie reached over and switched it off.

Leda darted a black look at Jennie and turned the radio back on. She kept her fingers curved around the knob. "I want to listen to the news."

Jennie tried to keep her tone light. "Do we really need any more bad news right now?"

"Some of us like to be informed."

Jennie glanced at each of the faces reflected in her

rearview mirror. Everyone was alert, attuned to the budding disagreement. Martha's eyes were no longer closed; they were fixed on the space in front of her. *Anything I say will make it worse.*

The commercial ended. The perky voice resumed, "Our lead story is breaking news," and became serious as it continued. "The police have just revealed that Leonard Atkinson, one of the educators murdered at a local restaurant, left his previous position in River County under a cloud." A long and dramatic pause followed.

The silence in the car was a physical presence, as real as ten extra pounds around the waistline.

Martha receded further into her corner.

Everyone else leaned forward.

The newscaster went on, "Mr. Atkinson reportedly was dismissed for supplying illegal substances to students. It is not clear if he was ever charged with a crime, but our sources say the alleged activity occurred over a long period of time and in a variety of different locations."

The words had the effect of a fingernail on a blackboard. This time it was Leda who turned off the radio.

Jennie shifted, giving herself a view of the other faces in the vehicle. All except Martha's registered embarrassment. Hers was . . . Jennie couldn't decide what her expression meant. Relief? Maybe.

No one spoke for hours it seemed, though probably less than a minute.

Martha finally broke the spell. "Now you know." She took a long, deep breath. "Now everyone will know."

Jennie said, "No one can blame you for your husband's actions."

No one responded to this, not even Martha.

The news must be over by now. Jennie turned on the radio again. The air was filled with a lively, jitterbug tune from the forties. Not really her first choice in music, but better than the quiet. Three songs and no conversation later, she pulled into Riverview's parking lot. She helped the ladies out of the van. They lined up on either side of the door. The effect was that Martha had to run a gauntlet of tea ladies to reach her car.

Faye put an arm around Martha's shoulders and said, "No one blames you, dear. Come see us whenever you need someone to talk to."

The other ladies echoed the invitation. They had evidently decided Martha was a lost lamb and were offering to be her shepherd.

Jennie felt like a proud mother. How could she have doubted them?

Martha mumbled, "Thanks," and fled.

After she drove away, Jennie said to Leda. "I'll be in to check on Doreen in a minute."

She kissed each of her ladies on the check, then turned to Elizabeth. "I guess I'll be seeing you tomorrow."

"Tomorrow? Oh, lunch."

Jennie nodded, asked, "Want me to drive?"

"That would be nice."

They walked together to the edge of the parking lot and arranged a meeting time.

Motion across the alley caught their attention. Ward Norris was exiting the restaurant. There was no sign of Lilly.

Elizabeth called, "Hello," loud enough for her voice to reach him and waved when he looked toward her.

He waved back and waited as she hurried across the alley.

Jennie watched. *What are they talking about?* Body language told her it was serious, whatever it was. Elizabeth did most of the talking. Twice, Ward shook his head as though answering "no" to a question. At one point, they both glanced up toward the porch overlooking the parking lot. *They're nervous about Lilly seeing them.*

Jennie considered ambling over to join them. She was pretty sure her presence would not be welcome. *All the more reason to do it.*

"Jennie." Leda made the decision for her. "I thought you were coming in to check on Doreen."

"I am. I'll be right there." A last look across the alley and a little promise to Ward. *Later.*

The chatter and distinctive tones of the tea ladies' voices floated out to Jennie as she approached Doreen's room. She came to the doorway just in time to hear, ". . . something we should investigate," in Georgie's husky warble.

Doreen was seated at the work table next to her easel, cleaning brushes. The movement of white cloth over limber bristles was delicate, almost a caress. The smell of paint thinner permeated the air. She wore an oversized man's shirt, stained with colorful daubs. She wasn't looking at Georgie, but her head was tilted in listening mode.

Jennie crossed the room and kissed Doreen on the cheek. "You okay?"

"Yes." Doreen reached for Jennie's hand. "Thank you."

Jennie studied her. No one would have guessed she had just lost the person closest to her. Jennie held fast to

Doreen's hand and turned to the others in the room. "What do you plan to investigate?"

There was an almost imperceptible change in their faces. They moved closer together and stood facing Jennie. No one answered.

"No investigating. The police know how to do their job." It occurred to Jennie that she sounded like Goodley as she waited for a reaction. There was none, a sure sign, she knew, of passive resistance from this group. She admired their style, if not their judgment.

Doreen broke the mood. "Jennie, I could use some help in planning Ann's memorial service."

"Of course."

Faye said, "I'd be happy to help too."

Doreen smiled at her. "I appreciate the offer, but we're not a religious family."

Faye smiled back. "I understand." She patted Doreen's shoulder and left.

The others follwed, leaving Jennie and Doreen alone.

Doreen removed her hand from Jennie's grasp and said, "I'm thinking about Thursday, day after tomorrow."

"Okay."

"I want to keep it simple." She spoke without meeting Jennie's eyes and with no inflection.

Jennie sat down on the bed and turned the wheelchair so they were face to face. "Are you sure you're okay?"

"Of course."

"Would you like to talk to someone?"

"I don't need grief counseling if that's what you're suggesting."

"It is. And I think you do."

Doreen turned to stare out the window. "I grieve privately." She spread her hands and, finally, looked Jennie squarely in the face. "That's how I am."

Experience had taught Jennie not to press for more than the older woman was ready to share. "If you change your mind—"

"You'll be the first to know." She favored Jennie with a smile. "Now, back to this memorial service. I cope by doing."

Jennie left Riverview after sharing a light lunch with Doreen in her room and headed toward the drugstore. She had no idea what she would say to Ward or, for that matter, if she had the right to say anything. But the conviction that he and Elizabeth were plotting behind Lilly's back was too strong to ignore. Jennie remembered Lilly's statement that she'd been getting pressure from both Elizabeth and Ward to accept Constance Barlow's offer. *Is that why Barlow invited Elizabeth to lunch tomorrow? Probably. But why include me?*

She pushed this question to the back of her mind when she saw a prime parking spot in front of the drugstore. Inside she was greeted by a young woman in a white jacket with Norris's Pharmacy embroidered in red over a pocket. "May I help you?"

"I'd like to speak to Mr. Norris."

"He's—"

Ward stepped from behind a partition with a professional smile on his face. When he saw Jennie, the smile slipped. He glanced toward the young woman. "I'll take care of it." He opened the half door separating the pharmacy counter from the rest of the store. "Come on back to my office."

Jennie followed him through a corridor lined with shelves crowded with bottles and packages, and into a tiny room. Fluorescent tubes filled the space with harsh light. There were no windows. The only furniture was a metal desk and two wooden chairs. On the wall above the desk were three framed photographs—one of Lilly and the three girls. Another, its colors faded, showed Ward and another man, the late Charlie Wainwright, with Lilly between them. The third photograph, obviously a school picture, showed a teenaged boy with a sullen expression. Jennie's gaze lingered on the this. She asked, "Is that your son?"

"Yes."

"Handsome boy. How old is he?"

"Fourteen." Ward's tone was flat, with no acknowledgement of the compliment to his son's good looks. His whole demeanor was artificial, almost robot-like. He held out one of the chairs for Jennie. When she was seated, he settled himself on the edge of the desk, towering over her. "You wanted to speak privately with me?"

Did I say privately? She groped for a reason for her visit. "I have a question about a prescription one of our residents is taking. Possible side effects, I mean."

"The name of the medication?"

Why didn't I think this through? Waiting for inspiration to strike, she opened the tote bag which served as a purse. "It's in here somewhere." She peered into the depths of the bag and moved objects around, then looked up at Ward. "That's not true. I wanted to ask what you and Elizabeth were talking about in the parking lot earlier today."

He'd taken off his glasses and was holding them by

one earpiece, dangling them above the hard floor while he studied Jennie.

She lifted her chin and went on, "I admit it's none of my business, but Lilly's a good friend and she doesn't have any family close by."

"You don't consider Elizabeth Lilly's family?" His eyes bored into hers.

"They're close, but it's not the same as blood kin."

"Maybe blood doesn't mean as much to Lilly as someone born in the South. Not everyone takes it as seriously as we do." He cleared his throat and put his glasses on. "I'm glad of this chance to speak with you. To apologize."

"Apologize?"

"For the other day, when I was at your home."

"You mean Saturday?"

"Yes."

Jennie waved it off. "We all have our good and bad days."

"Lilly and I . . . uh . . . had a disagreement. I had no right to take it out on you." His stiff manner was gone now. He seemed, if not vulnerable, at least human. "She's at a crucial point in her life. It's important she make the right decision." He stopped, looked at Jennie, as though waiting for her to comment. When she did not, he went on, "You have more influence with her than you may realize."

Jennie realized she was pleating her skirt between her fingers and forced her hand to be still. "I don't know what you're getting at."

"I'm sure you know there's been an offer to buy the house, a very generous offer. She should accept it."

"That's her decision."

"I know, but you could guide her."

"It's more than a house to Lilly. It's her livelihood. Hers and the girls. Elizabeth's too. And it's the only home she's known since she left the islands."

"Elizabeth agrees with me."

"Is that what the two of you were talking about in the parking lot?"

Instead of answering the question he said, "The happiness of that family means a great deal to me. Everything, in fact." His voice caught on the last words. His eyes were moist behind the thick glasses.

He and Jennie stared at each other.

Ward broke the silence. "I want to take care of them." The huskiness in his voice was more pronounced now. "I can do that. I can make them happy." At this moment Ward Norris looked like a man obsessed.

Chapter Twenty

Jennie knew it was Tom before she picked up the phone. "Hi," she said. "How's Seattle?"

"Rainy. How about Memphis?"

"Not bad. It may snow later. Kids are all excited. Hoping they won't have school."

It was a routine established early in their marriage, one they hadn't abandoned after the separation. When he was traveling, Tom called to check on Jennie and the kids as soon as he woke up. Sometimes she got a little prickly and pointed out he didn't need to know her every move. Fortunately, this morning her more reasonable self prevailed. Despite their differences, the one thing she and Tom agreed on was the importance to the kids of their maintaining a cordial relationship.

"They okay?" he asked.

"Fine. Tommy aced another math test."

"That's my boy. How about Andy?"

"He's good. Struggling with his spelling words, but hanging in there."

"As long as he keeps trying."

"I should say I'm struggling with his spelling words. He couldn't care less."

He laughed. "They're great kids. At least we did one thing right." A short pause. "Make that two."

"Yeah, we did." She thought of Lilly's battles with Jasmine and added, "So far anyway."

He laughed again. "Anything else?"

"Can't think of anything."

"What about the murders?"

"Police still haven't solved them." She saw no reason to tell Tom about Atkinson. He didn't need to know she'd uncovered that piece of the puzzle. Not that she regretted it, but she knew he'd have plenty to say about any involvement on her part.

Lunch with Constance Barlow and Elizabeth Wainwright was the last thing Jennie wanted to do with her day, especially if the weather bureau was right about the snow. It wouldn't be more than an inch or two, but that's more than drivers in Tennessee usually had to deal with. She tried to think of a way to wiggle out of the commitment. An image of Leda's chiding face took shape in her imagination. *I'd rather deal with the snow.*

What to wear? She looked through her closet, then out the window into the gray sky and settled on jeans, a fuzzy turtleneck, and a wool blazer. She dug out her down jacket to toss in the back seat. At least she wouldn't freeze if they got stuck somewhere.

By the time she picked Elizabeth up, snow was

falling. Huge flakes hovered and danced in the air before settling onto the street and disappearing.

She didn't pay much attention to the road signs, just followed Elizabeth's directions, but when they turned onto a familiar gravel road, Jennie realized the route to the Barlow farm was almost identical to the one she had traveled two days ago when she'd visited Martha Atkinson. "I didn't realize Constance Barlow lived so far out in the country."

Elizabeth said, "Her family's been on this land for generations."

"Tell me about them. I seem to be the only one who doesn't know their story. I know Leda's impressed."

Elizabeth smiled. "Most people are. They're horse people."

"Ah, horse people. Spelled m-o-n-e-y?"

"Lots of it. Enough you don't have to think about how to make more."

They passed Atkinson's rundown farmhouse, and Jennie remembered Martha telling her she was renting from Constance Barlow.

"How much of this land do they own?"

"Probably everything you can see."

"No wonder Leda's impressed."

"Yes."

Something in Elizabeth's tone told Jennie she must be thinking of the acreage the Wainwrights had once owned. She glanced at her passenger, but, as usual, the older woman's face revealed nothing. Jennie asked, "Was Constance born a Barlow or did she marry into the family?"

"Oh, she's a Barlow. To the core."

"Is she married? Did she keep her own name?"

"She's married. Or was. I've never heard her called anything but Barlow, so I guess she did."

"Where's the husband?"

"I don't know. She married when she went up north to college. A small wedding. No fuss and folderol. Not at all what you'd expect from that family. She brought her new husband back here a year or so later. Then he disappeared."

"Just disappeared?"

"As far as I know. Anyway, she's on her own."

"Any kids?"

"A son who's more interested in horses than people. At least that's what I've heard."

Jennie was pondering this, wondering if any of it mattered, when Elizabeth pointed to a pair of brick pillars and said, "There it is."

Jennie steered TBT through the columns. The driveway, bordered by white fences, was long and straight, until it curved into an oval in front of the house. A graceful veranda and tall columns supporting a wrought iron balcony seemed to say "Welcome, but wipe your feet." The scene looked more Kentucky horse-country than west Tennessee.

Jennie said, "I should have changed out of my jeans."

Elizabeth gave her an appraising glance—"You look fine, dear,"—and fingered the crease in her own wool slacks.

One of the doors opened before Jennie could ring the bell. A short, muscular woman, dressed in a maid's uniform, greeted them. "Mrs. Wainwright? Mrs. Connors?"

Both Jennie and Elizabeth nodded.

"Follow me," the women said. She spoke with a slight accent. Bobby pins secured a starched cap to wiry, russet-colored curls.

Jennie and Elizabeth followed her through a hallway lined with glass trophy cases. Framed photographs rested beside most of the trophies. Jennie slowed to get a better look at the pictures. Most showed a young boy, always either atop a horse or holding on to the bridle of a horse. A left turn took them through an elaborate formal dining room and into the adjoining sunroom.

Constance Barlow was waiting for them in front of a wall of multipaned windows. She smiled as they entered and beckoned them over. "Come, let's take a minute to enjoy the snow."

Elizabeth went to stand with their hostess by the windows.

Jennie lingered in the doorway and surveyed the room. The overall effect was inhumanly pristine. Jennie fought the urge to add a dirty fingerprint.

Barlow waved Jennie in, then nodded toward the maid, who turned and scurried off.

Jennie moved to the window and looked out on more Christmas-card unreality. Light snow was beginning to cover the gentle roll of land. Half a dozen horses frolicked. One, with a dark blue blanket on its back, moved with jittery daintiness, tossing its head and cantering in circles. An enormous white barn stood back about a hundred yards from the house, the same barn Jennie had seen from Martha Atkinson's kitchen window. Beyond the horses and the barn, she saw the farmhouse.

"That's where the Atkinsons live. Right?"

Constance turned to her with an arched eyebrow. "You know them?"

"Not Mr. Atkinson," Jennie said, "but I met Martha when she dropped by Riverview with a relative of one of our residents."

"When was that?"

"A few days after her husband's death." *Why do you care?*

Barlow studied Jennie through narrowed eyes. "How did you know where she lived? Did she tell you they were tenants of mine?"

"Yes, when I visited her the other day."

Barlow's expression clearly asked, "Why?"

Jennie said, "I dropped by to offer condolences and see if she needed a shoulder to cry on." *It's not quite a lie. I did offer her my friendship. No need to tell her more.*

"Oh," Barlow said. "Were you aware of her husband's, uh, history?"

"I heard about that on the radio, coming home from the funeral." Again, it wasn't quite a lie.

Elizabeth broke in. "Yes, it was very awkward. Poor Mrs. Atkinson was with us and was mortified. None of us knew what to say."

"I can well imagine," Barlow said. She kept her eyes on Jennie. "I didn't realize Martha went to the funeral with your Riverview group. I don't remember seeing her there."

"She left before the service was over," Jennie said. "She didn't feel well."

"That's odd. She visited me yesterday afternoon and she seemed fine."

Jennie said, "I guess the funeral upset her. The whole, uh, situation."

"Situation?"

"Her own husband's death. The fact they were both murdered."

Constance was still studying Jennie. "Well, it was nice of you to befriend her." She paused to laugh. "Actually, I'm trying to help her out too. I've hired her as a secretary. That's why she came to see me yesterday—to ask if I had a job for her. I've never employed a secretary before, though heaven knows I have enough paperwork to keep one busy." She turned around when soft footsteps approached. "Ah, here's Olga with lunch. I hope you like quiche."

Both Jennie and Elizabeth said, "Yes."

They seated themselves in accordance with Barlow's instructions and watched Olga place a tray filled with food on a nearby table. She served spinach salad onto translucent plates and set one before each of them.

Barlow said, "That's fine. I'll serve the quiche myself when we're ready."

Olga nodded, then disappeared.

There was a brief quiet before Barlow said, "These murders must be upsetting to both of you also."

Elizabeth said, "Yes, murder is bad enough when you see it on the evening news, but when it happens in one's home . . ." She let the sentence trail.

Barlow turned to Jennie. "And you? Were you working at Riverview that night?"

"I was there. Not exactly working."

"Still you must have seen all the excitement."

"Not really. I had my kids with me, and I tried to keep them away." *She invited us here to gossip?*

A timid cough saved Jennie from having to say more. She looked up to see Martha Atkinson. "Oh, hi. Good to see you again," Jennie said.

Martha nodded in Jennie's direction and spoke to Barlow. "You have a phone call."

A deep furrow appeared between Barlow's eyes. "Yes?"

Martha was quick to add, "It's your son."

Barlow rose quickly. "Excuse me. I'll just be a minute." She turned halfway out of the room and said, "Perhaps you could help yourselves to the quiche."

In the considerably more than a minute she was gone, Jennie and Elizabeth finished their lunch. Jennie began to wonder if the boy was sick and needed to be picked up from school. "How old is her son?" she asked Elizabeth. "Do you know?"

"I think about the same age as one of my grand-daughters."

Barlow came back while they were discussing this. "Sorry it took so long."

Elizabeth said, "I hope everything's okay."

"Oh, yes." Barlow offered no further explanation.

Jennie asked, "How old is your son?"

"Fourteen."

"That's the age of my granddaughter, Fleur," Elizabeth said. "I was just telling Jennie I thought he was the same age as one of my girls."

Jennie looked toward the windows. "Are they dismissing school early?"

"Not that I know of," Barlow said. "Bradley doesn't go to school here. He's at boarding school in Florida."

Jennie tried to imagine life without Tommy and Andy. "You must miss him."

"Yes, but the school here was just not suitable and I found a lovely place near my mother. They have dinner together at least once a week."

Why not suitable?

Elizabeth said, "That's nice for both of them."

Barlow smiled. "Ready for dessert?"

Olga must have been hovering nearby because she immediately appeared with a tray laden with three small compotes, each containing a perfect pear swimming in a golden sauce.

Why not suitable? Jennie couldn't get the question out of her head. *Did Barlow know about Atkinson?* Polite or not, she had to ask. "Did you know Leonard Atkinson supplied steroids to his athletes?"

Barlow sat very straight. "As a member of the School Board, I'm not at liberty to discuss the matter."

The School Board? Is she the one who gave Wyandotte the letter to sign? "Isn't it, um, unusual to be on the board in this district when you send your child away to school?"

Barlow responded with a tight-lipped smile.

Jennie felt a blow to her ankle and realized Elizabeth had delivered a sharp kick under the table.

When Barlow finally answered, it was clear she chose her words carefully. "I suppose it does seem unusual. I'm in a position to provide the best for my son. I serve on the School Board with the hope of raising the level of River County education for the benefit of those less fortunate."

Elizabeth smiled, nodded in obvious approval.

Jennie said, "How long has—is it Bradley—been going to the school in Florida?"

"This is his first year."

Again, Jennie knew it was rude, but asked anyway. She drew her feet under the chair, placing her ankles out of Elizabeth's range. "Because of Atkinson?"

"No. Bradley's at an age when I have to consider college. Make sure he's prepared."

Martha appeared again, this time carrying a box. She excused herself profusely and asked, "Where would you like me to put these?"

Barlow waved to the adjoining dining room. "On the table in there."

Martha disappeared without making eye contact with Jennie.

"Those are the pictures I was telling you about," Barlow said. "We'll look at them when we finish lunch."

They took their coffee into the dining room and spread the pictures out on the table's polished surface.

None of the faces staring out of the photographs looked remotely like any of Jennie's Riverview charges. "Which are the ones you thought I might be interested in?"

Barlow and Elizabeth were too busy studying a picture of two children, a little girl and a slightly taller boy, to answer Jennie's question. Elizabeth said, "I remember the day your mother took this. Charles was absolutely dreadful. He went off and left you to play on your own. I gave him a good talking-to about it when you left."

"I didn't mind," Barlow insisted.

"It must have been boring."

"I don't remember it that way."

Jennie thought Barlow was a little uncomfortable with the conversation.

If Elizabeth noticed, she gave no sign. "You did seem to enjoy exploring the house. We hardly heard a peep out of you all afternoon."

Restless, Jennie went to check on the snow. It had become heavier. When she returned to the dining room, she caught the tail end of a remark by Barlow: ". . . always willing to negotiate." *That's why she invited Elizabeth to lunch. Not just to gossip about the murders. She really wants that house. But why include me?* Jennie didn't care as much about the answer to the question as she did about getting home. "I hate to break this up, but we should leave. I'm afraid they'll dismiss school early, and I won't be there when the kids get home."

Barlow summoned Olga. While they were waiting for her to return with their coats, she said, "Jennie, do your boys like horses?"

"Don't all kids?"

"Yes, I guess they do. Would you like to bring them out to ride ours? With Bradley away at school, they don't get as much attention as they used to."

"They'd love that."

"Let's make it soon. I'm judging a horse show in Paducah this weekend. Perhaps next Saturday?"

"Thanks. I'll call to make sure it's still good for you."

Jennie kept a straight face, but she couldn't help but wonder about the real reason for the invitation. She couldn't think of a reason in the world for Constance's sudden interest in her.

Chapter Twenty-One

Jennie pulled into the parking lot of the funeral home, wheeled the van into a handicap space, and went to remove Doreen's chair from the back. The other tea ladies waited while she helped Doreen into her chair. Their faces were solemn. Not surprising. This was their second funeral in three days. And this death was closer to home than Phillip Jeffries' had been. The ladies might squabble among themselves, but when one of them hurt, all shared the pain. Besides, they'd all known and liked Doreen's niece, Ann. And her composure under the fire of their questions on her last visit to Riverview had added to their regard.

The funeral director met them at the front door and escorted them to the room reserved for Ann's service. They entered a high-ceilinged room decorated in multiple shades of lavender. Jennie felt like she was drowning in a sea of weak grape juice. Rows of straight-backed chairs, lined up with military precision, faced the front, where an urn rested on a small table. Doreen positioned herself at the entrance to the room. The ladies, with more decorum than they usually displayed, seated themselves in the back row of chairs, ready to offer support to Doreen in any way they could. Jennie stood by Doreen's side. Since they'd come early, in the interval reserved for family members, it was quiet for the first hour, an hour that seemed like at least six. By the time other mourners began to arrive, the tea ladies were restive and Doreen looked exhausted. She perked up, at least outwardly, when she began greeting people, many of them strangers to her, known only through Ann's accounts.

Jennie remained by Doreen's side, watching her, marveling at her composure. During a lull, Jennie whispered, "How about a little break?"

"No, I'm fine."

The whoosh of air brakes and the clammer of less subdued voices called Jennie's attention to the front door.

A school bus stood outside the entrance. Kids from the junior high where Ann had taught spilled into the lobby. Jennie looked for Fleur and saw her standing by the door, watching the parking lot. She disappeared, then reappeared with her mother and Jasmine.

Jasmine ignored propriety and pushed her way through the line to Doreen. Tears glistened in the tough teenager's eyes. "It's not fair."

Doreen held out both hands to the girl. "You're right," she said. "Sometimes life isn't fair, but I believe it evens out in the end."

Jasmine began to cry in earnest. Between sobs she said, "It wasn't supposed to be this way."

The line of people waiting to speak to Doreen came to a standstill. A woman in a navy silk suit, whom Jasmine had elbowed past, moved first. She nodded at Doreen, then hurried into the room, her lips pressed into a tight, disapproving circle. Others followed, eddying around Doreen, Jennie, and Jasmine.

Lilly approached and put a hand on her daughter's shoulder.

Jasmine shook herself free.

Fleur said, "Let me handle it, Mom." She put her arm around Jasmine's waist and guided her toward the restrooms. "Let's go wash your face."

Lilly took a step as though to follow, but stopped, her own eyes full of tears.

Jennie debated who needed her most, Doreen or Lilly.

Faye hopped up, took Lilly's hand in her own, and said, "Come, sit with us."

Jennie watched her lead Lilly to the row where the other tea ladies sat. They shifted to make a place for her in their midst.

A discrete tap on the shoulder distracted Jennie.

The funeral director looked meaningfully at his watch.

She held up two fingers and whispered, "Two minutes?"

He nodded and glided toward the front of the room.

Jennie leaned down to whisper in Doreen's ear, "How about that break now?"

This time Doreen agreed. "Good idea," she said, and turned her chair in the direction taken by Jasmine and Fleur.

"Um," Jennie said, "there's another restroom near the front door."

Doreen gave her a shrewd look. "So we can avoid running into Jasmine?"

"Yes."

"I want you to know I genuinely like that girl." She thrust her chin out. "And I don't believe half the things people say about her."

"I know," Jennie said, "but wouldn't you rather deal with her another time?"

"Um."

So they proceeded toward the restrooms near the entrance.

Ward Norris came in as they approached. He acknowledged Jennie's presence with a smile and concentrated on Doreen. "I was so sorry to learn of your niece's death." He spoke with a stilted precision.

"Thank you," Doreen said.

Leda was standing near the door when Jennie and Doreen returned to the main room. Everyone else was already seated. The tea ladies and Lilly had moved to the front row. Georgie reached over to straighten Lilly's collar.

Jennie took a moment to watch. Her ladies might be gossipy, sometimes downright nosey, but when the chips were down, they came through. She could imagine the signal that must have passed among them as they decided Lilly needed a little clucking over. They all loved Lilly, but Doreen was the only one who could see the scared kid behind Jasmine's bravado. *Speaking of Jas* . . . Jennie looked for the dark head. She wasn't there. Neither was Fleur.

"Are you going in?" Leda nudged Jennie. "Everyone's waiting."

Jennie helped Doreen to her spot, then went to the lectern and read from Emerson's essay on character. "Character is nature in the highest form. It is no use to ape it . . ." She paused to look up and saw Fleur standing alone in the doorway. Flustered, Jennie looked back at the book and read automatically, with no awareness of the words. Finally, she came to the end of the marked passage and returned to her place beside Doreen.

A middle-aged man with a gentle face and a sparse, graying ponytail replaced her and began reading from Thoreau.

Unable to concentrate, Jennie turned and looked over the heads of the other mourners. Fleur was still standing in the doorway. She crooked her fingers, beckoning Jennie. Jasmine was not with her.

Jennie looked toward Lilly, back at Fleur.

Fleur shook her head.

Jennie pointed to herself and raised her eyebrows.

Fleur looked relieved and nodded.

"Excuse me," Jennie whispered to Doreen.

Doreen didn't seem to notice.

Leda, on the other hand, darted a questioning look Jennie's way.

"What's up?" Jennie whispered when she joined Fleur.

"I need help. Jas is freaking out."

"Where is she?"

"Back there."

The room to which Fleur led Jennie was smaller, cozier, a haven from the formality of the rest of the place. Ward Norris and Jasmine stood, toe to toe, in the middle of the space, glowering at each other.

"Stay away from my mother," Jasmine hissed.

Ward said, "You have no reason to hate me."

"I never said I hated you. I just don't want you hanging around all the time." The decible level rose with each word Jasmine spoke.

"Your father—"

"Yeah, yeah, yeah, I know. You and my dad were best friends. So now you think you can take over his family. Why don't you go back to your own? Your kid could use some help. Leave us alone."

Ward's face was ashen. His arms hung at his sides, fingers clasping and unclasping.

Fleur began to cry softly.

Jennie stepped between Ward and Jasmine. "This is not the time or place."

Ward moved back.

Jasmine held her ground, but redirected her anger toward Jennie. "You think you have all the answers."

Leda appeared at the door. "Are you aware that voices carry in this building?"

Jennie looked at Ward, silently appealing to him to leave.

He swallowed as though preparing to say something, but turned and fled without speaking.

Even after he left, the room seemed filled with an electrical charge. Jennie looked at the two girls, wondering how to defuse the situation.

Fleur swiped at the tears on her cheeks and said to Jasmine, "Let's both wash our faces and go back in there."

Jasmine followed her sister to the door marked

LADIES. She half-turned as they passed Jennie and said, "Mom doesn't need to know about this."

Left alone, Jennie and Leda stared at each other. Leda finally said, "This seems to be your week for leaving funerals early."

Jennie's nerves were too raw to let it pass. "I distinctly remember you waving at me to get Martha out of the church the other day. And just now, Fleur asked for my help. Would it have been better if I'd ignored her?"

Leda heaved a huge sigh. "Conflict just seems to find you." She stretched her diminutive frame to its full height and clasped her hands in front of her. "And I do not like conflict."

"Then you're in the wrong business. You need to find a job that doesn't involve people."

Leda squared her shoulders and managed to add another inch of height. Her eyes glinted behind the rimless glasses.

Jennie knew she'd gone too far. A flash of inspiration told her how to recover. "By the way, did I mention that Constance Barlow invited me to bring the boys to the farm to ride her horses? Think I should go?"

"By all means." All hint of disapproval was gone, replaced by the glint of dollar signs.

Chapter Twenty-Two

Jennie coaxed one last bite from her apple and dropped the core in the trash. Lunch was over. Her desk was clear. No phone calls to return. Time to stop stalling and face the lioness in her den.

She paused just long enough for a quick wave when she passed the residents' dining hall on her way to Leda's office and complimented herself that, for a change, she had resisted the temptation to let herself be sidetracked.

The executive director's door was partway open. Jennie tapped on the frame and entered.

Leda, who'd apparently eaten lunch at her desk too, looked up. "Oh, Jennifer, hello."

Jennie chose to ignore the wary look on her boss's face. "I just wanted to let you know I'll be out of the building most of the afternoon."

The wary look threatened to become a frown.

Jennie said, "I'll be at Lilly's. The first quilt class is tomorrow. We're finalizing plans. If anything comes up, you have my cell phone number." She smiled and waited for Leda to respond in kind.

She didn't. Her mouth remained a straight, firm line, which seemed not to waver even as she spoke. "Try to stay out of the Wainwright family problems. At least don't bring them back to Riverview."

"I promise to be on my good behavior."

"Um." Never had Jennie heard a single syllable convey such doubt.

She shoved the doubt and her promise to the back burner when she crossed the alley to Lilly's. She needed to concentrate on the task ahead. *I have to tell her. Everything.* Since she'd telephoned to let Lilly know she was on her way, she didn't bother to knock, but retrieved the spare key hidden among the vines on the arbor and let herself in.

By the time Jennie was on the second step, Lilly appeared. She stood at the top, looking down at Jennie. "Okay, what happened?"

"Happened?"

"Yesterday. At the service. That little set-to between Ward and my girls."

"I came in on the tail end of an argument between Jasmine and Ward."

"About what?"

Jennie waited until she reached the top before she answered. "She warned him to stay away from you."

Lilly's gaze didn't waver. "How bad was it?"

Jennie bit her lower lip.

Lilly's fingers fluttered, coaxing details from Jennie. "Come on. I want the whole story. I'm tired of being the last to know what my girls are up to."

"You know how Jasmine feels about Ward." Jennie wondered how to say what had to come next. Straight out is best. "She told him to stay away from you."

"She said that?"

"Loud and clear. She even told him to go back to his own kid."

Lilly looked a little dazed. After a minute, she asked, "What about Fleur?"

"She watched, but didn't say much. Did you ask them about this?"

"Yes, last night. They stonewalled me. I did everything I could think of to get them to talk. Nothing worked. They both clammed up. No arguments. No defiance. Just that wide-eyed Mom-we-don't-know-what-the-big-deal-is look." While she spoke, Lilly prowled the room, moving with restless energy from one piece of furniture to another. She stopped in front of the sideboard and picked up a photograph of Jasmine as a toddler. She sighed and touched one finger to the chubby face in the picture before setting it back down and resuming her pacing.

Jennie said, "Look, whatever else happens, sooner or later, you have to deal with Ward."

Lilly spun away and took long strides across the room. "I am dealing with Ward. There's not a day that goes by he doesn't call or drop by."

"So tell him to stop. Say it like you mean it." Jennie cringed at the pain in her friend's eyes, but didn't back down. "Level with him about your feelings." She paused, picking words with care. "Maybe first you need to level with yourself. Because I'm picking up vibes—"

"Don't say that." Lilly's whispered words came out as a plea.

Jennie steeled herself and went on, "You have a right to your own life."

"It's more complicated than that. Jasmine hates him. She'd be furious."

"More furious than she already is?"

Lilly didn't answer that. She gathered her long hair in one hand and held it off her neck, as though the weight were more than she could bear. "You're right. I need to be decisive. The uncertainty is too much for . . . all of us." She released her hair, let it cascade down her back in a long ripple, then added, "Except Charly. She's the one bright spot. It's hard to believe the way she's handling everything. It's almost as if she's oblivious to it."

Jennie knew she had to betray her son's confidence. "That's not true. She thinks Jasmine killed the two men at your restaurant. That's what she told Tommy."

Lilly looked like she'd been punched in the stomach.

Jennie put her hand on Lilly's shoulder. "I'm sorry. I didn't want to tell you that."

An electronic buzz startled both of them. Jennie fished the cell phone out of her tote bag and checked caller ID "Weston Goodley." She pushed the button. "Hi, Wes."

There was an audible intake of breath before he said, "Our dinner last week got interrupted. Care to try again?"

"I've got the kids this weekend."

"How about a movie? One they'd like."

"I want to do something with just the kids. Something normal. Kind of an antidote to everything that's going on."

"I understand. Rain check?"

"Sure."

"Speaking of the murders, that's partly why I hoped we could get together. I'd like to talk to you about something."

A charge went through Jennie. "What?"

"Don't get all excited. There's no big, new development." A long pause, then, "Be careful, okay?"

"Why do you—"

"Maybe we can get together early next week. In the meantime, no playing detective."

"But—"

He cut her short again. "I'll call you. Right now I have to get back to work. Be careful."

She closed the phone, intrigued. Her thoughts darted in fifty different directions. *I could call Tom. Ask if . . . ohmigod, I'm actually thinking of giving up time with the kids. He's right. I'm too caught up in this.* She looked up and saw Lilly staring at her.

Lilly wagged a finger in Jennie's face and smirked. "You need to take your own advice."

"I don't know what you mean."

Lilly crossed her arms in front of her. "Yes, you do."

"Wes?"

"Um hmm."

"I told him I'm not ready for anything serious."

"Does he believe you?"

"Who knows?" She tried to shake off the question

Lilly had raised and replayed the phone conversation in her head. "He wanted to talk to me about the murders. He said, 'speaking of the murders,' and I hadn't mentioned them. Then he told me to be careful. He said it twice."

Lilly was looking again at the pictures on her sideboard. When she turned around, she said, "He's been talking to the Memphis police, and they've been talking to the people at Riverview." She lifted her chin. "I know some of them think Jasmine killed Jeffries and Atkinson. The police have probably made the connection about your and Ann's cars being so similar. Wes knows you spend a lot of time over here. He's warning you about Jasmine."

"There could be another explanation."

"Could be, but I don't think so. After I found out Jas had threatened you, I talked to Georgie. A lot of people overheard the argument. Most of them believe she's capable of anything."

"I don't."

Lilly leaned toward Jennie, accusing her. "You believe she sneaked out of the house that night and lied about it."

Jennie was tempted to say what Lilly wanted to hear, but she stuck to her guns. "Yes, I do. But that's not the same as believing she'd murder someone."

"Bottom line, though, you don't believe her. I do. I don't know who you saw, but I'm sure it wasn't my daughter." She looked hard at Jennie. "Have you told the police about that?"

"No. I'm going to, though."

"Please don't."

"Why? If you're sure it wasn't Jasmine?"

"I figure the police will add that to everything else they've heard and assume it was her. So they won't really investigate. At the very least, they'll start asking my girls a lot of questions and make things worse for us . . . if that's possible."

"But if she's innocent—"

"Not if, Jen. Jasmine has her faults, but she's not a murderer. Most people . . . all they see when they look at Jasmine is anger. They don't understand the reason for it."

"Do you?"

"Not completely, but . . . Jas is like her father was. She can't compromise. She's afraid of Ward—not just Ward, anybody—taking Charlie's place. I think that threatens her own identity. So she lashes out. People see that and they think she's capable of anything, even murder. I don't want the police any more suspicious than they already are. I don't share your faith that truth always wins out. Besides, I believe her when she says she wasn't on the balcony."

"Okay, let's say it wasn't Jasmine I saw. Who was it? And what were they doing upstairs? How'd they get in?"

"It could have been anyone. There were a lot of people around that night."

"But, Lilly, if it wasn't Jasmine, it must have been the murderer. If we can figure out who it was, this'll be over."

Lilly rubbed her forehead as though to iron out the worry lines. "Please, Jen, humor me."

"I won't say anything unless I have to. That's the best I can do."

"Thanks. It's more than I have a right to ask."

Jennie shook off Lilly's gratitude. She said, "Enough about that. We haven't even touched on the reason we got together. The quilt class starts tomorrow. Are we ready?"

Lilly shook her head. "I'm sorry. I have to cancel. I'll give everyone their money back."

"Don't be silly. That's why I came over. To help get ready. What do we have to do?"

"A lot. I haven't even had time to shop, so I don't have what I need to begin."

"Okay. That's our starting point. We'll take them shopping tomorrow. They'll love it. Do you know where you want to go?"

"There's a woman on River Road, a little over a mile north of here, who has a shop in her house. She dyes her own cloth. Gorgeous stuff. Her fabrics look like Bali prints, but they're a lot cheaper, and perfect for what I have in mind."

"Wonderful. No more talk about canceling. Agreed?"

Lilly took her time, but she finally said, "Agreed."

Jennie glanced at her watch. "Kids'll be home soon. I better go." Before she left, she hugged Lilly and said, "Sorry if I pushed too hard."

"Don't apologize. It takes a friend to tell you the hard truths. I'll talk to the girls. Lay it all on the table. I'll do it tomorrow."

"Not tonight?"

"No. And don't look at me like that. I'm not putting it off. Elizabeth's going to Little Rock to spend a few days with her cousin. She's leaving bright and early in the morning. After the quilt class, we'll have the rest of the weekend to ourselves."

"Perfect opportunity." Jennie started down the steps, had an idea and turned, "Why don't you and the girls have dinner with us tonight? Let Elizabeth pack in peace?"

Lilly looked tempted for a minute, then shook her head. "You don't want to cook for everybody. You've had a tough day, too."

"Who's cooking? I'm talking pizza. As in takeout."

Chapter Twenty-Three

"I don't see why we have to pick up our room just because Charly's coming."

"Andy, cut it out. You're cleaning your room because it needs it."

"I didn't invite her."

"You want to close the door and spend the evening in this messy room while the rest of us have a pizza party?"

Tommy put in his two cents. "Sounds good to me. I'd let him."

Andy wouldn't give up. "We're just gonna get stuff out again."

Jennie didn't feel like debating the merits of tidiness. "Enough. I have a phone call to make and a couple of things to do. Five minutes. That's how long it's going to take. When I come back, there better not be a Lego in sight."

Two sulky faces looked up at her.

Lighten up, Jen. They're kids. She changed her tack, adopted a deep, mock-stern voice, and added, "And do you know what I'm gonna do if there is?"

The boys' expressions brightened, reflecting the humor they detected in their mother's tone.

Andy, still a little wary, said, "No."

"I'm gonna order anchovies on the pizzas."

Andy laughed, then groaned. "No way!"

Tommy clutched his chest and keeled to the floor.

Jennie laughed with them and stretched her arms. "Come on, triple hug."

Both moved forward into her arms.

She kissed the tops of their heads, savoring the earthy, boy-child scent of them, more pleasing at this moment than the most exotic perfume. Before she let them go, she said, "Help me out, guys. The Wainwrights need a little cheering up. Let's make tonight a good time for them."

The lighter approach helped. Tommy went to work on the Legos and Andy concentrated on a pile-up of Matchbox cars.

She went to the phone in the kitchen to call Doreen to inform her about the change in plans for tomorrow morning.

Doreen's response was enthusiastic. "A shopping expedition. Everyone will like that."

"You'll let them know?"

"Yes."

"Thanks. I wouldn't ask, but Lilly and the girls are coming over tonight, and I'm trying to get things in order."

"I'll see everyone at dinner anyway." There was a long pause before Doreen asked, "How's Jasmine? Have you seen her today?"

Jennie was caught off guard by the question, especially by the too-casual tone in which Doreen had asked it. "I haven't seen Jasmine. I talked to Lilly earlier, when we made our plans. Why?"

"No reason. Just making conversation."

"Come on, I know you better than that. What's up?"

"Nothing's up. At least nothing I know about, but she's been preoccupied the past couple of days. I worry about her. She's not nearly as tough as everyone thinks."

Jennie waited for Doreen to add more. When she didn't, Jennie said, "If you knew anything, you'd tell me, wouldn't you?"

"Of course."

"Even if it meant you had to violate a confidence?"

"Jennifer, I am not a child. Please don't speak to me like I am."

Jennie tried to make amends. "I'm sorry. I didn't mean it like that."

"I know." The edge disappeared from Doreen's voice. "I guess we're all a little nervous these days. I'll relay the message, and we'll see you in the morning."

"Right. Bye." She held the phone a few seconds, mulling over the flare-up. It was so totally unlike Doreen, Jennie felt certain something must have prompted the question about Jasmine.

She was still puzzling over Doreen's inquiry when the doorbell rang. As expected, Lilly and the girls were on the doorstep.

Charly held up the latest *Harry Potter* video.

Lilly had a tray of kabobs made from chunks of pineapple and spongecake with chocolate drizzled over them.

Jasmine and Fleur lagged behind. Neither looked glad to be here.

Fleur at least tried. "Hi, Mrs. Connors. Thanks for inviting us." She smiled and reached to hug Jennie, her half dozen bracelets setting off a silvery jangle.

Jasmine rolled her eyes and swaggered in.

Lilly looked tired, on the point of collapse.

Jennie bussed her cheek and whispered in her ear, "Don't worry about it." She took the tray. "This looks heavenly. Maybe we should skip the pizza and go straight to dessert."

After Jennie ordered the pizzas, Lilly said, "We can't stay too long. I promised Jasmine and Fleur they could go to a late movie with some friends."

"Fair enough." *In other words, you bribed them to get them to come.*

Lilly must have read Jennie's mind because she said, "Just wait. Tommy's nine. Your turn's coming."

The pizzas, sans anchovies, were better than average and Lilly's dessert was every bit as good as it looked. When both were finished, Charly asked, "Can we watch the video now? I heard it's really good."

Jennie's boys were making like bobblehead dolls. "Yes, yes, yes!"

She glanced at Lilly and the older girls. "They can watch it in my bedroom. I have another idea for us."

Jasmine and Fleur exchanged looks.

After Jennie settled the kids, she returned to the

kitchen juggling a book, a bottle of nail polish remover, some cotton balls, and a shoebox containing all the old nail polish she'd been able to rummage. "Anyone for a pedicure?"

The silence was thunderous.

Jennie appealed to the girls. "Come on, humor your mother and me."

She lay the book on the table. The words *Far-Out Nails* were spelled out on the cover by photos of fingernails decorated in an assortment of colorful designs.

"I tried to do this." Jennie pointed to a pale pink nail embellished with a daisy. "Complete disaster."

Fleur smiled.

Jasmine rolled her eyes. Again.

Jennie realized the tactics she used with Tommy and Andy weren't going to work with these girls. She started over. "Okay, so it's silly. Can't we just forget about the rest of the world for a couple of hours and do something silly?"

Honesty worked where manipulation had failed.

Jasmine picked up the book and started flipping pages. When she looked up at Jennie, she almost smiled. "I'm game."

Two minutes later, they had their shoes off. Jasmine took charge, creating miniscule designs with a few deft brushstrokes. The other three gave up in awe, watched, and waited their turn for her to work her magic.

Jasmine and Fleur loosened up to the point where they began chatting about plans to take a new girl in Jasmine's class to Mud Island the following day.

Lilly interrupted, "We agreed to spend tomorrow together."

The girls exchanged alarmed looks.

"Your grandmother will be gone, and we can talk about some of the things that've been going on. There are a lot of loose ends dangling. We need to talk about them. All of us."

Fleur said, "But you have your quilt class. And Charly has swim team practice."

Lilly said, "Right, but we still have the afternoon. You two sleep in on Saturdays anyway."

Jasmine was adamant. "Mom, we made plans."

Lilly was equally so. "You'll have to change them."

Fleur said, "This is important to us."

"Not as important as family matters."

Jasmine thumped her fist on the table, knocking over a bottle of blood-red polish.

"Jas!" Lilly sounded at the end of her rope.

Jennie grabbed a roll of paper towels and swiped at the mess. "No harm done."

Fleur shot her sister a let-me-handle-it look, then concentrated on their mother. "You're asking us to let our friends down."

"No, I'm not. I'm asking—telling you—you have to spend tomorrow afternoon at home with Charly and me." Lilly's jaw was set.

Jasmine, calm again after the outburst, said, "Why this sudden togetherness thing? Do you have any clue what's going on?"

"I'm trying to find out."

"You don't have to ruin our day tomorrow. I'll tell you now. That Atkinson creep offered illegal drugs to Fleur's friends. Guys on the football team."

Lilly opened her mouth, looked ready to speak.

Jasmine held up her hand, silencing her. "I'm the one who went to Mr. Jeffries and told him about it." She paused and nodded in the direction of her mother and Jennie. "Yeah, it was me. He tried to put me off with the usual 'I'll take care of it crap,' but I didn't trust him. I threatened to call *The Commercial Appeal*."

Lilly asked, "What did he say to that?"

"He wanted me to let him talk to Atkinson. I told him he better do more than talk." Jasmine pounded her fist into her palm. The resounding *thack* made everyone wince. "I told him I'd kill both of them if he didn't keep Atkinson away from my sister and her friends." She stopped to look at her mother. "Now you know. I threatened them and now they're dead." She stood and rolled her shoulders as if a weight had been lifted from them before she went on. "Anyway, he still said he had to talk to Atkinson before he took any action. He invited the slimeball to dinner at our restaurant so I could see him do it. That's why I was down there in the kitchen that night." Tears welled in her eyes. She swiped at the tears and drew herself up. "That's why Jeffries and Atkinson were there." She puffed her cheeks and blew out the air. "I saw them. Dr. Jeffries caught my eye and nodded. So I went up to my room." She looked at Jennie. "And I stayed there."

Fleur said, "That's right. I was with her."

Jasmine shook her head at her sister. "No, you weren't. You don't have to lie for me." She looked at her mother and repeated, "I stayed in my room. When I heard all the commotion, I figured it was probably Atkinson denying he did anything wrong and arguing with Dr. Jeffries. I knew you'd be upset about a scene in our restaurant. I didn't want you to know I had anything to do with it, so I stayed in my room and acted like I didn't hear anything. But I promise I didn't go out on the balcony and sneak out." She turned a furious face to Jennie. "I don't care what you think you saw."

"I don't just think I saw someone. I did. They, whoever it was, climbed over the railing. It was dark, so I can't actually say I saw them climb down the arbor, but," she spread her hands, "what else would they do?"

Jasmine looked at her with her chin thrust forward, but didn't venture an opinion.

Lilly said, "I'm sure you saw someone, but I'm confident it wasn't Jasmine. And whoever it was . . ." The unfinished thought hung in the air: was probably the murderer.

"Talking about it won't change anything." Fleur's tone was patient and much too world-weary for a fourteen-year-old.

Jasmine went back to the previous argument. "So, can we go with our friends tomorrow?"

Lilly stood firm. "No. Whether it changes anything or not, we have to talk. About a lot of things."

A look passed between the the two girls.

Jennie glanced at Lilly to see if she noticed. It was hard to tell.

The girls didn't say anything but it was clear they hadn't given up.

Then, without warning, Jasmine's sullen expression changed. "Can we still go to the movies tonight?"

Lilly said, "Okay. Just remember you promised to come straight home after."

"Sure." Jasmine excused herself to go to the bathroom. On her way out of the room, she said over her shoulder, "Some day I'm going to just take off. New Orleans, here I come."

Lilly watched her walk down the hall and said to Fleur, "Why didn't you tell me about Atkinson offering your friends drugs?"

"He didn't offer them to me, so what difference does it make?"

"It matters a lot when you don't come to me. We have to change that."

"I know, Mom." Fleur, the peacemaker, crossed the room and put an arm around her mother.

Lilly pulled her closer. "My little rock. Do me a favor. Don't let Jas do anything crazy. Some day this will be over."

"I know. Maybe sooner than you think."

Jennie perked up. "What does that mean?"

"Nothing special. Just . . . it's gotta end sometime."

Another emotional day. Thank God it's almost over. Jennie listened to the boys bicker while they brushed their teeth and steeled herself for one more confrontation.

After kissing Andy and helping him arrange his pillow just right, she said, "Tommy, we need to talk."

Andy sat up. "Don't you want to talk to me?"

"Another time. You can hardly keep your eyes open now."

He half-smiled and snuggled under his quilt without argument.

Thank you, thank you, thank you, God.

Tommy followed her into the family room.

She sat on the couch and took both of his hands into

hers. "I told Lilly today what you told me about Charly. That she thinks Jasmine killed those people."

His stricken face was like a nail in her side.

"I had to do it. That's too big a secret to keep."

"You promised!"

"No, actually I didn't. I said I wouldn't tell if you didn't want me to."

"I thought it was a promise."

"I know. So it's like I did break a promise. And I'm so sorry." She went on, "I thought a long time about how I'd feel if you had a big secret like that. I know I'd want to be able to talk to you about it. Don't you think Charly needs to talk to a grown-up about this?"

He seemed to consider and finally nodded his assent.

"I think so too, and I believe you've been a good friend to Charly by telling me so I could tell her mother." She watched a series of conflicting emotions flicker across his mobile face, bracing herself for an argument.

Finally he said, "It's okay."

"Good. I'm really glad you understand." She rose from the couch and took his hand. "Now, bedtime. Big day tomorrow."

"What're we gonna do?"

"For starters, you guys have swim team practice. I'll take you. Daddy's picking you up, and he'll bring you to Riverview because Lilly and I are taking the ladies shopping. Then, after lunch, we'll do something special."

"What?"

"I don't know. We'll put our heads together and think of something."

Chapter Twenty-Four

The phone jolted Jennie from sleep. She reached for the receiver and, at the same time, glanced at the clock. One forty-seven. This can't be good. "Hello."

"The girls aren't home." Lilly's words ran together, so indistinct it took Jennie a minute to process them. Not so, their tone. Panic came through loud and clear.

"They're probably with friends and lost track of time."

"That's not it. Jasmine, maybe. Not Fleur. She doesn't do this."

"What time was the movie over?"

"Eleven-thirty."

"Do they have a cell phone with them?"

"Of course. I've been calling every fifteen minutes since midnight. It's turned off."

"That doesn't mean anything. They had to turn it off when they went into the movie. They probably forgot—"

"They've run away."

"Oh, come on, didn't you ever miss a curfew?"

"You're not taking this seriously." Lilly's panic was escalating.

"I am, but—"

"Jasmine said she was just going to take off. Don't you remember?"

Jennie did remember. That had been her first thought, but she'd tried to push it away. Lilly didn't need to hear that. What did she need? *Something useful. Think of something useful.* "Have you called the police?"

"No. I called all the hospitals. Nothing."

"Okay, at least you know they haven't been in an accident."

"It's just like Jasmine to run away."

"But Fleur wouldn't. You know that."

"I asked Fleur to try to keep her sister from doing anything foolish. If Jasmine decided to take off, this is exactly what Fleur would do."

Jennie couldn't reason that away. "Do you want me to come over?"

Lilly expelled a loud breath. "No, I know you can't. The boys are asleep."

"I can wake them." Even as she said it, Jennie dreaded the thought of hustling the kids out of their beds and into the cold night.

"Don't. There's nothing you can do."

"Is Elizabeth there?"

"No. When the kids and I got home we found a note. Her cousin came by early, and they decided to leave tonight instead of in the morning."

"I'd feel better if you at least had a car."

The sound of measured breaths came through the phone.

Jennie said, "I'm sure they're fine."

"You don't think Jasmine took off like she said, and Fleur went along?"

"No. I think they ran into friends and the time got away from them."

"If that's all it is, I'll kill them . . . but, dear God, I hope you're right." Lilly was obviously still worried, but her panic was under control. "Thanks, Jen."

"For what?"

"For being someone I can call in the middle of the night. For listening. Go back to bed. I'll wait here."

"Call me if you hear anything. Or think of anything I can do."

"No matter when?"

"Do you have to ask?"

"No."

Jennie replaced the phone and burrowed deeper into the nest of covers. She willed herself to sleep. It didn't work. She couldn't stop imagining what Lilly was going through. She tried to convince herself the teenagers had run into friends and were cruising around Memphis, listening to tapes and complaining about their parents. That didn't work either. Jasmine's over-the-shoulder "New Orleans, here I come" remark wouldn't let it.

She switched on the light and sat up, pulling the blanket around her shoulders. She reached for a magazine and started flipping pages. She soon gave up on that, got up, went to the kitchen, and filled the kettle.

While she waited for the water to boil, she stared at her reflection in the dark window panes and tried to sort out the past week's events. Everything seemed to swirl around Jasmine. Had she really run away? No, Fleur's much too sensible to let her. But there's just so much a younger sibling can do, and if Jas was determined to leave, Fleur would stick with her. Like the twitch of a cat's tail, Jennie's thoughts moved from "No, they'd never do that" to "That's exactly what they've done."

This isn't helping. She tried to force her thoughts to other possibilities, but couldn't help thinking, *Jasmine isn't one to make idle threats. What about her threat to me?* This brought her to Doreen's conviction that Ann Tull had been murdered. Was she right? And, if so, was it because her car so closely resembled Jennie's? Was Jennie herself in danger? She didn't think so.

She'd even begun to doubt it was Jasmine she'd seen on the balcony the night of the murders. She remembered feeling the intruder was looking at her. What if she was right? What if the intruder thought she'd seen something and could identify her? Or him? It had been a tall person.

Jennie made a mental list of people she knew had been at the restaurant that night. Martha Atkinson. Constance Barlow. Ward Norris. Two of the three had sons the right age to have obtained steroids from Atkinson. Martha didn't, but just being married to a guy like that was motive enough for murder.

Why had Wes warned to her to be careful? Did he know something he couldn't share? Another route that led back to Jasmine. What if the murderer had known exactly whose car they were doctoring? That would mean Ann was the intended victim. That was more likely. The only link between the three victims was Hillcrest Junior High School.

Steroids. Jennie was no expert, but she knew they could cause personality changes and extreme anger. Extreme anger—another path that led back to Jasmine. How many kids had said yes to the steroids? And what about their parents? If Mrs. Wyandotte was telling the truth, they'd been content to shuffle Atkinson off to another school district rather than deal with an unpleasant situation. It had taken Jasmine to meet the problem head-on.

Jennie wondered who else knew about the meeting Jasmine had forced between Atkinson and Jeffries, a meeting that had led to both their deaths. Against her will, she wondered if the girls' disappearance had anything to do with those deaths.

Stop it! Not everything is related to the murders. The girls were upset they had to cancel their plans. Maybe they decided to punish their mother. That'd be just like Jas. But not Fleur.

"Mom." Tommy's hand was on her shoulder. "The kettle's whistling like crazy."

She jumped up and turned off the burner. Had she really been that lost in the maze of her thoughts? Apparently so. "Did it wake you up?"

"Yeah."

"I'm sorry. Come on, let's get you back to bed. It's the middle of the night."

"How come you're up?"

"I couldn't sleep."

"Didn't you hear the kettle?"

"No. I . . ." He deserved an explanation. Should she tell him about Lilly's call? No, best not to go into that. The thought of someone running away from home would set his nine-year-old imagination aflame. She settled for half the truth. "I was thinking about Lilly and her family, hoping this will be over soon."

"Me too."

She pulled him close and buried her face in the soft fluff of his hair. "I know you do. Charly's lucky to have you for a friend."

"Um," was all he said. He looked at his mother a few seconds. "You should have that special tea like Grammie drinks. The kind that makes you sleepy."

"Good idea. How about you? Think you can get back to sleep?"

"I guess."

She went with him, tucked him in, and returned to the kitchen for a cup of Celestial Seasonings' Sleepytime.

The tea didn't work. She spent the rest of the night huddled in a tall wingchair with a book, hoping a puzzle created by Agatha Christie would distract her from the very real problem confronting Lilly. She finally slipped into a fitful doze and woke immediately when the phone rang at 6 AM. She grabbed it. "Lilly?"

"They're still not here."

"No word at all?"

"No. I called the hospitals again. There haven't been any accidents."

"The police?"

"I called them fifteen minutes ago. They won't do anything until they've been missing for twenty-four hours." Lilly sounded frighteningly calm.

"I'll wake the kids and come right over."

"No. Don't."

"Why?"

"I've had all night to think about this. Did you mean it when you said you'd do anything you could to help?"

"Of course."

"I want you to take the ladies shopping. I'll give you directions. Don't say anything about the girls. I know everyone's suspicious of Jasmine, so I'd rather not have anyone know she's run away."

"You don't know she has."

"I know. I'm going to start calling all their friends. The police won't do anything until nine-thirty. I'm hoping by that time, I'll know where they're headed."

"You're sure this is what you want me to do?"

"Yes. I've had all night to think about it."

"What about Charly? Want me to take her to swim practice?"

"No. I want her here with me."

Jennie hung up, more spooked than she'd been when Lilly was hysterical.

Chapter Twenty-Five

The boys chattered nonstop all the way to the Y. Jennie managed to divide her attention between the hopscotch of their interests and the circuitous route demanded by her concern for the Wainwright family.

Tom was waiting just inside the door when they entered the building. "Want me to take over from here?"

She glanced at her watch. "I'll wait for you in the viewing area."

"I thought this was the big day for your quilt class."

"It is. I need to talk to you first, though."

"Oh?"

She glanced toward the boys, indicating she'd prefer a private conversation.

He nodded, showing he understood and went with Tommy and Andy to the changing room.

While she waited for Tom, Jennie thought about how best to explain the situation. *Better level with him. Com-*

pletely. He won't be happy, but— She'd just reached this conclusion when he appeared at the bottom of the stairs. She caught his eye and watched him ascend, two steps at a time, with the effortless grace of his track star days.

"What's up?" A furrow settled between his eyes, indicating that he'd picked up on her apprehension.

"It's about Lilly. Her girls, I mean. Not Charly. Jasmine and Fleur. They went to a late movie last night and didn't come home." She waited for him to tell her it was none of her business.

He didn't. Instead, he sat next to her. "What can I do?"

"I don't know. I'm not sure what I should do either. Lilly wants me to go ahead with the quilt class. She'll call me if she hears from the girls. In the meantime, I'm taking the ladies to buy fabric. When we get back I'll check with Lilly and see if anything's changed. I should probably stay with her."

"Do whatever you need to. I'll keep the troops occupied. Call me if you hear anything."

Jennie gulped back tears. "Thanks." She inclined her head toward the pool area. "They don't know about it. Nobody does except me, and now you."

"She didn't call the police?"

"Yes, but it's too soon for them to get involved. Lilly asked me not to say anything to anyone else. People are so quick to believe the worst of Jasmine, she's afraid this'll just be more fodder for the gossip mill. Jasmine threatened to run away, and Lilly's afraid she's done it and Fleur went along."

For a few seconds they watched their sons at the pool's edge. Tommy was all concentration, listening to the coach. Andy was at the other end of the pool with the younger children, horsing around with two other boys.

Tom put his hand on Jennie's. There was no need for either of them to say what they were thinking. They were united in the prayer they sent up for the safety of Lilly's girls and, by extension, the security of their sons.

The Riverview van was waiting by the ramp. A sedan with NORRIS PHARMACY painted along its side was parked at an angle two slots over. Jennie squeezed between the two vehicles, annoyed by the inept way the car was parked. Probably some kid who's had his license all of two weeks. Inside, she put this out of her mind and headed for the activities room. When she entered the room, she found Ward Norris waiting.

"Hi," she said and waited for some explanation of his presence. When there was none, she said, "I have to make a phone call."

"To Lilly?"

"No. This is . . . well, actually, it's kind of private." She looked toward the door. "You mind?"

"Of course not. Sorry." He started to leave, turned back. "Lilly's coming here, isn't she? Doesn't that class she's teaching start this morning?"

"Yes, but she's, uh, not feeling well. I'm on my own today."

"Lilly's sick?"

"Just a little under the weather." She glanced at her watch, willing him to leave before the ladies came.

He didn't take the hint.

"Uh, do you need something from me?"

"No. I was just making a prescripton delivery and

thought I'd stop in and say hi to Lilly." He started to leave, but turned back. "Did she say anything about the girls?"

"Why would she?"

"No reason. I just thought after, uh, Jasmine and I had that fight at the funeral, uh . . ." He seemed tight as a coiled spring.

He doesn't make deliveries. He pays a kid to do that. She cleared her throat, said, "I'm, um, kind of in a hurry." She looked again toward the door.

Finally he left.

The encounter gave Jennie goose bumps. She tried to reason them away. *There's nothing wrong with him delivering prescriptions himself. I've never seen him so jumpy though.* She picked up the phone and punched in Goodley's home number.

"Hi, it's me, Jennie," she said when he answered. She went on without giving him time to say anything. "Yesterday, when you called, why'd you tell me to be careful?"

"Nothing special. I know you think you have to be involved in these murders because of Lilly being your friend. That could be dangerous."

"Why for me specifically?"

"You're not exactly keeping a low profile."

"Do you think it's dangerous for other people too? For instance, Lilly's girls?"

There was a hesitation before he answered. "What's this about?"

"Look, I'm not supposed to say anything, but Jasmine and Fleur didn't come home last night. Lilly's afraid they've run away. I was wondering if maybe it's more serious than that. Not that that isn't serious enough."

A low whistle came through the phone. "Do the Memphis police have this information?"

"Lilly called them, but they told her they won't get involved until the girls have been gone twenty-four hours."

"That's standard."

Jennie waited for him to say more. When he didn't, she prompted, "They, I mean the police, didn't seem to make a connection with the murder investigation. At least Lilly didn't tell me if they did."

"Where's Lilly now?"

"At home, by the phone. They only have one car and the girls took it."

"Where are you?"

"At Riverview. I'll be leaving in a few minutes, though. I'm supposed to take some of our residents shopping this morning. Lilly wants me to act like nothing's wrong."

Goodley didn't say anything.

Jennie said, "I'm not even sure why I called you. I keep trying to reassure Lilly, but, to tell the truth, I've got a bad feeling about this. I thought maybe you'd have some advice."

"The same advice I've given you all along. Stay out of it. I'll call the officer in charge of the murder investigation. If I find out anything, I'll call you. If I can, that is."

"Thanks. I know I'm asking for more than I have a right to."

He chuckled. "I didn't think I'd ever hear you admit that."

"Here she is, girls." Georgie's throaty voice intruded.

"I'll do what I can, but listen, I meant it when I told you to be careful." Goodley was dead serious again.

"I know. Look, I have to go. My ladies are here. You can reach me on my cell phone." She turned to the six elderly women gathered near the door, their bright faces demanding no less than her full attention.

"We've been waiting for you by the door. Thought you forgot about us. And here you are, dawdling on the telephone like a teenager."

Georgie's scolding tone provided a curious relief to Jennie. At least something was normal.

"Well, I'm ready to go now." Jennie picked up her tote bag and turned off the light on her way into the hall.

Doreen said, "Lilly isn't here?"

"Uh, no. She's not feeling well. We're on our own."

"What do you mean, she's not feeling well?" Georgie obviously expected a more detailed account.

"I meant exactly what I said. She's picked up a bug or something." Jennie put on her most honest face and tried to keep it light.

Doreen was more subtle, but no less insistent. "Nothing serious, I hope."

"I hope so too." Jennie quickened her pace. "I have to run over and get directions to the fabric store, then we'll be all set. Meet you at the van." On her way out, she stopped to ask an aide to help Doreen into the van and to load her chair.

Outside, she was surprised to discover Ward hadn't

left yet. He was standing beside his car, looking across the alley toward Lilly's place. His arms hung by his side, his fingers alternately clasping into a fist and stretching long, as though reaching for something. Jennie called out to him, but he didn't respond.

Anxious to be away from him, Jennie started across the alley, stopped when she heard her name called. She looked up and saw Lilly standing on the balcony.

"Wait there," Lilly called. "Charly's coming down with a map."

"Great. Thanks."

"I called ahead, told the shop owner what we're looking for. She has some pieces she thinks will be perfect. She'll set them aside."

Jennie wanted to ask about the girls, but didn't think Lilly would be willing to broadcast a status report to the neighborhood from her balcony, especially with Ward looking on. She settled for a coded message. "Feeling better?"

Lilly's answer was an ambigous waggle of her hand.

Charly darted out the door and ran toward Jennie. "Here's the map and a note from Mom."

Jennie unfolded the two sheets of paper—one was obviously a map, the other a series of numbers, measurements, it looked like, nothing about the girls. She quickly looked up at Lilly.

Lilly shrugged and shook her head. Even from this distance, she looked exhausted, ten years older than she had at dinner last night.

Jennie waited until she saw Charly re-enter the house and lock the door behind her, then crossed the alley to where the ladies were waiting inside the van with expectant faces.

This time it was Tess, usually the quietest member of the group, who spoke. "Lilly looked fine to me."

It's going to be a long day.

Chapter Twenty-Six

Jennie studied the map, then tucked it over the visor, started the van, and headed north. According to Lilly's directions, the shop was located in a brick farmhouse on Buck Run Road, three quarters of a mile east of River Road.

The terrain they traveled through was bottomland, flat as a blackboard and just about that color. Stubby remains of corn stalks poked through its level surface in straight rows. Periodically, a line of trees signaled the end of one field, the beginning of another. Homes were sparce and modest. The sky was cloudless, almost white in its brillance. The beauty of this landscape was not obvious or dramatic, but possessive of an asture dignity that testified to the character of its people.

Georgie was not interested in scenery, dignified or otherwise. She took up the question raised by Tess earlier. "Lilly didn't look sick to me either."

Vera tried to calm Georgie with a practical note.

"How could you tell? You only saw her from a distance. You know she wouldn't cancel without a reason."

"Yes, I do know that," Georgie snapped back, "but I'm not interested in a reason, as you put it. I want the truth." She leaned forward to tap Jennie's shoulder. "What exactly did she say was wrong?"

She's worse than Tommy. "She wasn't really specific. When I talked to her early this morning, she just said she'd been up all night and couldn't make it today. I didn't press for details." Jennie congratulated herself; she hadn't lied.

A quiet settled. Jennie's mind returned to Ward's unexpected presence at Riverview. She tried to remember the last time she'd seen him deliver prescriptions. Nothing came to mind. Certainly nothing on a Saturday. *He's busy in the store.* And that's when the kids are available. This reminded her of the manner in which the pharmacy's car had been positioned. Like an inexperienced driver had parked it. Or someone in a hurry. Or upset. Ward was upset all right. Staring at Lilly's back door like a lovesick teenager. *Why was he waiting for me in the activities room? What did he say? Oh yeah, something about saying hi to Lilly.*

A ring split the silence. Jennie reached into the tote bag for her cell phone. "Hello."

"Jennie, Wes here."

Her throat went dry. "You've heard something?"

"Uh, no. Just a question for you. What kind of vehicle were the girls driving?"

"Ford Windstar."

"What year?"

"I'm not sure. A couple of years old."

"Silver gray?"

"Yes."

"You know the license number?"

"No." Does anyone really know things like that? "Did you find the car?"

"I didn't say that." The next sound was the impersonal click of a disconnect.

Jennie threw the phone into the seat next to her.

A hush like a brick wall greeted her outburst.

She retrieved the phone, started to dial him back, but knew it would be useless.

Predictably, Georgie was the one to broach the silence. "Who was that?"

Jennie pulled over to the shoulder and stopped the van. "Give me a minute. Okay? I have to think."

She felt more than saw the looks exchanged. It didn't matter. Goodley knew something. Should she call Lilly and tell her? Tell her what? Goodley had mentioned a color, silvery gray, the color of the vehicle the girls were driving. Not a reason to call Lilly. Not yet. When Jennie asked if they'd found the car, Wes hadn't said no. That meant yes. Should she take the ladies back to Riverview, then try to find him? That would take at least half an hour. She either had to mind her own business and proceed with the shopping trip or take the ladies with her while she went looking for him. Not much of a choice. She'd probably never find him. And she had no right to involve the ladies in a wild goose chase. Jennie knew there was only one right thing to do. And she knew she wasn't going to do it.

She took a deep breath and half-turned so she was facing her passengers. "I'm going to level with you guys."

Six gray heads leaned closer.

"Lilly isn't really sick."

At least one tongue clicked. There was a whispered, "I knew it!"

"Her girls didn't come home last night. I mean the older two, Jasmine and Fleur."

"They've been kidnapped!"

"Is there a ransom note?"

"Lilly thinks they've run away." Jennie paused for another deep breath. "That phone call was from Lieutenant Goodley up here in River County. I called this morning and asked him to help me. And just now, he asked me what kind of vehicle the girls were driving."

"He's found it." Georgie sounded as certain as Jennie felt.

"I don't know. He wouldn't tell me."

"Where was he calling from?"

"I'm not sure. I'm guessing from a police car."

Doreen said, "And you want to try to find him and see if you can help the girls?"

Hearing it spoken aloud, Jennie winced. It was a dumb idea. Still, she couldn't force herself to turn back. "If it were my kids," was the refrain that kept playing in her head. She said, "I don't want to put you guys in danger."

Their arguments were swift and adamant. "How will we be in danger?" "We'll be with the police." "You can't get any safer than that." "Those girls will be glad to see us." "The police won't be much comfort to them."

Jennie let their comments swirl around her. "Okay," she said. "I don't know where he is now, but I can probably get the information from someone where he works."

"We're going to the police station." Tess sounded thrilled.

"Well, it's not exactly a police station," Jennie said. "It's the building where all River County government has its offices. I've been there and the receptionist, Ms. Dugan, knows me. I think I can convince her to at least tell me if they found the car. We'll take it from there."

The ladies put on properly solemn faces. Jennie knew their concern for Lilly's girls was genuine. That didn't dilute their excitement at the idea of an adventure.

She restarted the van and pulled onto the gravel road. She wasn't too concerned about danger. After all, as one of the ladies had said, they'd be with the police. Another thought did slow her down, however. She blurted it out without thinking. "I may lose my job over this."

"Leda will never know," Georgie said.

The other five were quick to agree.

"Hey, I don't want anybody to lie for me. This is my decision. I'll live with whatever happens. I just can't stand to think of what Lilly's going through. I want to find those girls and get them back home."

Faye said, "We feel the same way, dear. Don't worry about us. Sometimes a lie is justified."

Vera said, "Leda's not likely to even ask about it. Why should she?"

That made sense to Jennie. Sort of.

Chapter Twenty-Seven

The drive to the station took ten minutes. When she pulled in to the parking lot, Jennie spotted Goodley's gray Jetta in its usual spot. *So, he's either in the building or out in one of the patrol cars.* She looked around. There were no marked cars in sight. She pulled in to a slot marked VISITOR and turned to the ladies. "This'll only take a minute. You guys wait here."

Georgie was quick to suggest, "I'll come with you. You may want someone to take notes."

"It's best if I go in by myself."

"But—" Georgie started to protest.

Tess stopped her. "There's more at stake here than your ego."

The reference to Georgie's ego had the predictable effect. She bristled and glared at Tess.

Jennie mouthed a silent "Thank you" to Tess and opened the van door.

Inside River County's Administration Center, Ms.

Dugan was listening with a bored expression to a rail-thin gentleman, dressed in faded Levis and a plaid shirt. "My neighbor's assessment is half what mine is. And they've got a bigger house and twenty more acres." The line between his eyes grew deeper with each word.

"You'll have to talk to Mrs. Peterson. She's the assessor."

He craned his neck and looked at the sea of empty desks behind her. "Where is she?"

"She'll be here nine o'clock Monday morning." With that, Dugan moved down the counter to Jennie. "Help you?"

"I'm not sure." Jennie said. "I was talking to Lieutenent Goodley and my cell phone cut out. I think he wanted me to meet him somewhere and see if I could identify a vehicle."

Dugan's eyesbrows shot up. "An abandoned vehicle?"

"I think so. I missed a lot of what he said."

The irate taxpayer pushed himself in front of Jennie. "Excuse me, but I was here first." He leaned forward until his face was within inches of Dugan's. "I pay your salary, young woman. I'd like an answer about this." He lay a much-creased paper on the counter between them and gave it a sharp rap with his fingertips.

"Sir, I'm the receptionist. I don't know anything about what goes on in the departments."

"If you don't know anything, what're we paying you for?" He tapped the paper again. "That's why our taxes are so darn high."

Jennie could see the clock ticking away her chances of finding Goodley. She reached over the counter and lay her hand on Dugan's arm. "I got the impression the lieutenant was kind of in a hurry."

Dugan looked grateful for the interruption.

The taxpayer said, "She can't help you. She don't know what goes on in the departments."

If looks could kill, the one Dugan shot would have netted River County one less taxpaying citizen.

Jennie persisted. "You said something about an abandoned vehicle."

Dugan turned away from the man. "He must have meant that vehicle they found over near the Atkinson place."

"Atkinson. Yes, I think that's it. Thanks." Jennie gave her a wide smile. She figured the woman needed a little encouragement. The man with the tax problem looked like he planned to stick around.

When she got back in the van, Faye was humming "Blessed Assurance" while Georgie stared out the window with an expression more like "In the Bleak Midwinter." The other four ladies sat in carefully neutral poses.

"Well, did you find out anything?" Georgie was definitely snappish.

"Yep."

Faye stopped humming.

All six leaned forward.

"Well?"

"Goodley's gone to investigate an abandoned car. At least I think he has. Dugan had other things on her mind and didn't say much."

"Who's Dugan?"

"She answers the phone for everybody in the building."

"Did she tell you where the car is?"

"Not in so many words, but," Jennie paused for effect, "she mentioned the Atkinson place."

"Atkinson, as in Leonard Atkinson, the teacher who gave the kids drugs?" Georgie's eyes were like lighted Roman candles. "I know exactly what happened."

"I doubt that," Doreen said.

Georgie went on, undaunted, "Atkinson's wife finally got tired of his shenanigans and killed him. Jasmine and Fleur figured it out and went after her. She'd holding them captive somewhere."

Doreen wasn't convinced. "Somehow, I can't imagine Martha Atkinson doing that."

"Why not?"

"She seemed like such a timid little soul."

George glanced at Tess and said, "It's those timid little souls you have to watch."

Jennie let them go on with their bickering. Their ideas echoed her own. She knew Martha was sick of following her husband from school to school and, for some reason, wasn't willing to leave him. Georgie's theory was certainly a possibility. But not the only one.

She drove along the now familiar route to the Atkinson place trying to picture Martha as a multiple murderess. She was at the restaurant that night. Had she poisoned the two men, then sneaked up Lilly's back stairs and escaped down the arbor? Had she been the figure on the balcony that night?

Jennie tried to remember exactly how the scene had looked. Could someone else have reached the second floor? Martha seemed a likely candidate; she was the kind of figure people tended not to notice. On the other hand, like Doreen, Jennie couldn't see Martha committing murder. She weighed these competing notions while watching for police cars or any unusual activity along the route.

An abandoned car wouldn't be left in the open. The deer that had darted in front of her car the other day came to mind, the curve in the road just before Martha Atkinson's house. *I was coming from the south then. Going this way, it'll be after Martha's house*. The overgrown road she'd spotted seemed like a perfect place to hide a vehicle. *Hide a vehicle!*

If the girls had run away like Lilly suspected, their vehicle wouldn't be hidden. It would be barreling down I55 toward New Orleans. Maybe this was a wild goose chase. No one had mentioned what type of vehicle had been found. Actually they hadn't really even said they'd found one. Jennie had made a gigantic leap, based on the scanty information she'd gleaned from Dugan. Well, she'd come too far to turn back now. Much too far. Just ahead, she saw the Atkinson house.

"There's where Martha Atkinson lives," she said.

Georgie said, "It could sure use a coat of paint."

Jennie slowed, looking for any sign of life. Nothing. She noted that the *T* and the *I* were still missing from the name on the mailbox. The wooded area was just ahead. Within seconds they were at the entrance to the overgrown road. She stopped and peered into a tunnel formed by tall trees with bare limbs that reached out and intertwined. It was hard to distinguish solid forms from shadow. Jennie removed her sunglasses and could

see movement, people walking around, at least one vehicle. Without giving herself time to think, she turned
in. They bumped along about fifty yards before being
flagged down by a man in uniform.

"Where do you think you're going?"

Jennie recognized the cop everyone called Smitty
and lowered her window.

He recognized her too. "Lieutenant," he called over
his shoulder. "Guess who's here."

Goodley strode forward. He did not look glad to see
Jennie.

Too bad. At the moment that was the least of her
worries. She jumped out of the van and looked past
Smitty. Two police cars were pulled over to the side of
the lane, and a little further on, she saw the dark silhouette of another vehicle. Her eyes had adjusted to the
reduced light enough for her to recognize Lilly's Windstar.

She looked from the car to Goodley. "The girls?"

He shook his head.

Jennie was having trouble breathing. She leaned forward, put her hands on her knees, and took deep, slow
drafts of air. She straightened up, tried to form a question. "They're not . . ."

"I haven't seen them. Just the vehicle." His eyes met
hers. "You shouldn't be here."

"Just tell me if you think they're . . ."

"Dead?" He added the word she couldn't bear to say.
She nodded.

"No reason to think so. Footprints lead over there."
He pointed deeper into the woods in the direction of the

river. He took Jennie's elbow and guided her back to the van. "I'm losing valuable time talking to you."

She climbed into the vehicle without protest.

"You want to help?"

She nodded.

"Then stay here."

"Maybe I—"

Goodley slammed the door shut and walked away.

The ladies clamored to know what was going on.

Jennie filled them in as best she could. "We have to wait here. We'll be in the way if we try to follow them. Might even endanger the girls." She expected an argument, at least from Georgie. There was none. And nothing to do but wait. She zipped and unzipped her jacket.

Someone's stomach growled.

Jennie glanced at the clock on the dash. Almost noon. Lunch at Riverview was served promptly at eleven-thirty. She fished in the tote bag and brought out three cellophane packets. Not much, but better than nothing. "Anybody for a peanut butter cracker?"

All insisted they couldn't eat a bite, but the crackers disappeared.

Time stretched. No sign of Goodley. Or the girls.

The food, scant though it was, triggered the after-lunch-nap impulse in the ladies. Not so, Jennie. Adrenalin made it impossible for her to remain in the van. She eased open the door.

All six heads snapped to attention.

"I'm just going to stretch my legs," Jennie said.

Even Georgie looked alarmed. She said, "Are you sure it's safe?"

"I'm not going anywhere. I just need to walk around a minute."

Doreen seemed to understand. "Stay close, dear."

"I will. You guys, stay here. You look like you could use a little down time." She kept her tone light.

Their faces showed that they weren't fooled, but no one argued.

She had no plan in mind, but felt drawn to the Windstar. It was cold in the shadow of the overhanging trees. She shivered and wrapped her scarf closer around her neck. The top layer of ground was frozen, but it gave way to a slushy softness when stepped on. A puddle in the center of the road was covered with a thin skim of ice. Jennie stepped into the woods to avoid it. A bright shimmer caught her eye. She bent to examine it. A sparkling silver hoop was half-buried in sodden leaves. A loop earring. Jasmine! The earring had to belong to Jasmine!

Chapter Twenty-Eight

She looked for Goodley, and when she saw him, called out, "I found something!"

If he heard her, he didn't acknowledge it. He and the two other policemen were walking in a line, shoulder to shoulder, heads down, nudging the leaves with the tips of their shoes. Murmured words drifted back, low tones, becoming less distinct as the three figures moved further away.

She called out again. "Hey, over here."

Still no response.

She wondered why Goodley had chosen to go the way he had. And how had the three professionals missed the earring? She reached for the silver loop. *Did they?* Maybe they'd seen it and left it there for a reason. She drew back her hand. *Procedure? He's big on that.*

She started after them, but stopped mid-stride. *They don't need my help. I'll follow a different path in case they're wrong.* She made a slow circle, looking for breaks in the underbrush that grew waist-high in most places. A maze of passageways zigzagged through widely spaced trees and low bramble. These paths were carpeted with leaves, wet and shiny, compressed and molded into a single sheet. A pattern of depressions filled with slushy water showed where deer and other animals had stepped. She looked for human footprints but didn't see any. On the path leading to the edge of the woods, another bright glint caught her eye. She went to examine it and found another earring, this time a bright silver stud. Again she resisted the temptation to pick it up. Instead, she stood where she was and looked at the earring, then back to where she'd found the silver hoop. Careful examination of the area showed broken sticks and leaves dislodged from the leafy mat. She saw no obvious footprint, just the prints left by the sharp hooves of animals. She reasoned that human feet were too large to penetrate the tight mat in the same way that dainty animal hooves would.

She looked back over the way she had come and drew an imaginary line from the first to the second earring. She turned and, with her mind's eye, extended the line. Another glint beckoned her forward. She followed its call and found a slender bangle bracelet. *That's Fleur's!* She was now at a fork made by two narrow lanes. She squinted down at each of them. No clue as to which she should take. The one to her left was a little wider. That seemed the more sensible choice, so she followed it, too absorbed in her quest to think about danger. She ducked under a vine that looped between two trees. A sharp tug at the back of her head stopped her. She tried to turn; the pressure increased. She put her hand back and discovered that her hair was caught in a branch. Untangling it was like trying to fasten a button that rests in the small of your back. She finally gave up, snapped the branch on both sides and left it there. She walked slowly, conscious of the movement of the object in her hair, always looking for some sign that the path had been used by other humans. After about ten yards, she realized there were too many unbroken sticks for the path to have been traveled recently by creatures as large as Lilly's girls. She retraced her steps to where the paths had forked and followed the narrower one. A tiny glimmer of light caught her attention. This time she found a silver stud lying on a flat rock.

"Yes!"

The sound of her voice startled her. Involuntarily, she put her hand to her mouth and looked around. The forest seemed dead except for bird sounds high above. She continued and found another stud a little further along. By now she had no doubt the girls were leaving a trail.

A broken branch intersected the path. She examined the ends where the limb had snapped and could tell the break was recent. Just ahead, the path split into a lopsided Y. Peering through the narrow passage of the shorter leg, she saw light. She chose this direction and followed it to where the tree line met a field. When she looked across the open area, she saw the back of a farmhouse. Martha Atkinson's place. She watched, alert for some sign of activity, but saw none. Quiet as a tomb. She shivered. *Bad analogy. Think positive.*

She took a step back, desiring the cover of the trees.

Okay, what next? Should I go get Wes? She chewed her lip, estimating how far she must have come. How far had Goodley and his men gone in the opposite direction? *It might take a while. Anything could happen.* She gave a wistful thought to the cell phone lying in the van. While she debated going back, she saw another glint of silver, where the path had split. A shiny object was wedged into the crook of a tree, just at eye level. She went toward it. Another bangle bracelet. There was no doubt it belonged to Fleur. The other leg of the Y continued through the wooded area, parallel to the field about ten feet from the tree line.

This trail was easier to follow. Trees were further apart; ground-level vegetation was thicker, but looked drier, more brittle. Signs indicated that someone had left the path. Bold-patterned footprints, such as would be left by a sneaker, were visible. A trampled area, surrounded by broken underbrush, indicated a scuffle. Jennie was drawn forward. *Just a little further. Then I'll get Wes. Maybe I'll have something to tell him. More than just a trail. I'll know where it leads. That'll save time in the long run.* The footprints led her out of the woods. She estimated she was about a hundred yards from where the other path had led. A gust of wind whipped her hair into her face, reminding her how exposed she was. She returned to the cover of the trees and looked in all directions. There was a clear pattern of disturbed earth leading to the barn she'd seen from both the Atkinson's kitchen window and Barlow's sun porch. On her right was the tenant's house; on her left, the landlord's home.

She started to turn around and go for help, but a

voice in her head stopped her. *Lilly's girls are in that barn. If I'm in danger, they're in danger. It's too late to go back.* She estimated the distance to the barn. About a hundred yards. Not far, but crossing the field, she'd be visible to anyone at either residence. She looked at the field of winter-dry grass. Her leather jacket would stand out against the much paler brown. An easy target.

She looked again toward the barn, checked the field for obstacles. A pitchfork pierced the side of a huge circular hay bale off to one side. But her course was clear. She took a deep breath and sprinted, looking neither left nor right. She was almost there when her knees buckled. She went down hard. She felt a jolt in her wrists, then a stinging sensation in the palms of both hands when she landed. She lay there a few seconds, not understanding why she'd fallen. A small rabbit hopped across the field and she realized she must have stepped into one of his holes. *Sorry, fella.* She ignored the throbbing in her ankle, got up, and kept going. Her breath was coming in ragged bursts by the time she reached the barn. No matter. She was there. She leaned against the back wall and allowed herself the luxury of slow, deep breaths. Her chest was on fire, but her head was clear. The two residences were closer to the road than the barn, so no one in either place could see her as long as she remained behind the barn.

Okay, I'm here. What next?

She'd cut herself off from Goodley. For better or worse, she was on her own. She continued to take deep breaths, sucking air into her lungs while she pondered this. She wondered if she'd been spotted. From her limited view, she didn't see anyone. The only movement in the field was the shadow of a hawk circling overhead. She felt a moment of pity for the rabbit who was probably crouching in the stubble. *Forget the rabbit. You've got your own problems!* Something distracted her. What was that? She concentrated on listening. Her breath was thunderous in her ears, but she was certain that's not what she'd heard.

The noise came from inside the barn. The girls? Some kind of animal? Jennie took her fist and rapped lightly on the barn wall.

The noises ceased.

She waited. The silence was unnatural. She knocked again, this time sending a definite pattern: *tap, tap,* pause, *tap, tap, tap.* She put her ear to the wall and listened.

After what seemed an eternity but was probably less than a minute, the taps came back with the pattern repeated.

She caught her breath. *No animal did that. Not the four-legged kind.* She moved to the end of the barn, to where the answering taps seemed to originate. "Jasmine?" She waited for an answer.

Nothing.

The taps sounded again. Same pattern. But she heard no words.

It doesn't have to be the girls. It could be anybody. What if it's a trap?

While she considered this, it occurred to Jennie that her voice hadn't been heard. Her throat felt frozen; she couldn't be sure she had actually uttered the name aloud. She tried again, this time taking a deep breath first, and enunciating clearly, "Jasmine."

"Who is it?'

That's her. "Jennie Connors."

"We need help. Hurry."

"Is Fleur with you?"

A softer voice answered. "I'm here. Please hurry."

"Can you—"

"We're tied up."

Chapter Twenty-Nine

J ennie leaned forward and tried to see if there might be a door on this side. No such luck. Three cautious steps took her to the corner. From this angle, the Barlow complex was visible. It lay across the field to the left, closer to the road than the barn. The hay bale lay in the sight line between the house and the barn, the only object that might block the view. Jennie saw the glassed-in area where she and Elizabeth had lunched with Constance only three days ago. Sunlight made black panels of the windows. It was impossible to tell if anyone was watching from there. There was no sign of activity either in the field or around the residence.

She gritted her teeth against the daggers of pain that shot upward with each step and kept moving. She leaned against the wall, supporting herself with her hands to ease the pressure on her ankle, and edged toward the front corner. The siding grated on her scratched palms. When she reached the corner, she paused for a deep breath. She saw the circling shadow on the field again and looked up, watched as the hawk swooped to earth, then re-ascended in an unbroken fluid motion. The squeals of the small creature in his talons pierced Jennie's heart like a baby's cry.

She took a quick look around the corner of the barn and saw no one. She checked the house again. *From that distance, no one can tell who it is anyway. Look like you belong here.* The door was in the middle of the barn face, only feet away. She left her flattened position against the wall and took the first step toward it. A jolt of pain from the ankle almost brought her down again. She bit her lip and limped her way to the door. When she reached it, she grabbed the heavy bar and tried to lift. It moved two inches, then stopped. She looked to the side, where the bar was resting in a piece of thick metal bent outward. An old-fashioned padlock, massive and heavy, dangled from a hole that went through both the bar and its resting place. The lock was not engaged. *Yes!* The relief that surged through Jennie's heart was enough to make her forget her ankle. Two steps sideways. She was in position to remove the lock, open the door, and be in the barn.

She thought she heard footsteps and glanced in the direction from which they seemed to come, but saw only the monolithic bale. She removed the lock and strained to lift the heavy bar. A shadow appeared and hovered over her—an elongated figure with hair that stuck out like bits of straw. Jennie bent her knees and shifted her shoulders for leverage to heave the bar upward. At the same time, she prepared to dive into the safety of the barn when the door swung open. The shadow advanced, darkening as it came closer. There wasn't time. She would have to confront the enemy. She watched the arms move; one seemed to extend, to rise in the air above the head. Thin, straight, long, with . . . what? The pitchfork. No confronting that. Jennie tensed, stopped trying to lift the bar, gathered her strength, and hoped her attacker didn't know they'd been spotted. She waited until she heard the footsteps clearly, the crackle of hay, the crunch of pebbles, an agonizing eternity that probably lasted ten seconds.

The padlock was still in her hand. She flexed her arm at the elbow to gauge its heft, at the same time keeping her eye on the silhouette. When it hesitated as though to steady itself, Jennie spun around. She crouched low, extended her arms, and swung the heavy lock. A jolt traveled up both arms as metal collided with flesh and bone.

"Ow!"

Jennie watched her attacker fall backward, arms flailing, then crash to the ground.

Constance Barlow lay, arms and legs outspread, limp as a rag doll. Her clothes were disarranged except for knee-high riding boots, which kept their martial stiffness. Blood streamed from a gash on her forehead.

Jennie watched, momentarily paralyzed, as the blood began a slow trickle down Barlow's cheek.

As though in slow motion, Constance rolled to one side and put both hands to her face. Red fluid oozed between pale fingers, incongruous and repulsive. Somehow, in all the maneuvering, Barlow managed to keep her eyes open and on Jennie.

Jennie had to look away. Her glance fell on the pitchfork, just inches from where her would-be attacker lay, within easy reach when she recovered from the initial shock of the blow. Barlow must have followed Jennie's glance because she reached for the pitchfork.

Jennie saw what she was doing and kicked it away.

Barlow rolled her body toward Jennie and grabbed for an ankle.

Jennie danced sideways. The bad ankle gave way and forced her to her knees. She stretched her arm and managed to retrieve the pitchfork. She concentrated on standing, gritting her teeth against the pain shooting up her leg from the ankle. She stood over the other woman, holding the tool aloft in both hands.

Barlow curled into a fetal position.

Jennie braced herself, gathering strength, then shuddered when the realization hit that she had been ready to propel the lethal tines into the flesh of another human being. *Not that. I can't do that. What then? Tie her up?* She looked around for a rope. There was none. She spotted a coil of wire lying near the barn door. She used the tines of the large fork to bring the wire within reach. Without letting go of the pitchfork, she picked up the wire. It was thick, stiff. Could she twist it into a knot? She'd have to.

"Turn over." She hardly recognized the snarling voice as her own.

Barlow curled into a more compact ball.

Jennie prodded her lightly and winced at the resulting whimper. "I said, turn over! On your stomach."

The only response was another, more mournful, whimper.

"I don't want to hurt you. But you can't leave."

"I won't. I promise."

Jennie didn't bother to say what she thought of a promise from someone who had, just seconds ago, tried to skewer her with a barnyard tool. She used that same weapon to nudge Barlow's side. "Over."

Barlow took her hands away from her eyes and stared at Jennie. "Why are you doing this?"

"I think it's called self-defense." She prodded her again. "Over."

Finally, Barlow complied. From her prone position, she tried a different approach. "I didn't know it was you."

"You attack any stranger who wanders onto your property?"

"I thought you were an intruder. What're you doing breaking into my barn?"

"I've come to get Lilly's girls."

"Lilly's girls?"

"I know they're in there." Jennie tilted her head toward the barn.

"I didn't know that. I certainly had nothing to do with it. Let me up. You'll need my help to set them free."

"Nice try." Jennie tossed the pitchfork toward the barn door, well out of Barlow's reach, then dropped to her knees. The woman started to roll back over, and Jennie stopped her by placing a knee firmly in the small of her back. She looked at the length of wire. *Okay, how do I do this?* She grabbed Barlow's wrists and tried to tighten the coil around them. In order to keep her knee in position, Jennie had to jerk the woman's arms up high. Barlow grunted as her chin was forced down onto the hay-strewn ground.

Jennie's fingers weren't strong enough to bring the wire snug. A gust of wind blew her scarf out and into her line of sight. She dropped the wire and managed to take off her scarf without letting go of her captive's hands. *That'll work.*

When the other woman struggled, Jennie ground her knee harder into her back and used the scarf to tie her hands together.

Barlow howled.

Jennie tried not to see the blood from Barlow's hands staining the white scarf vivid red, expanding outward until it reached the sides, darkening as it followed the hem line.

Barlow began to struggle again. She dug her knees into the ground and twisted her body. Jennie fell sideways. Barlow rolled to her side and kicked out with both legs. Jennie scooted away, just beyond the reach of the stiff leather boots.

I'll have to tie her feet too. Jennie scrambled upright and looked around for something other than the stiff wire. Nothing looked promising. Her eye rested on the pitchfork and she considered hitting Barlow with that to knock her out, but doubted she could do it. Then it occurred to her the pitchfork could be used to twist the wire into a tight loop around Barlow's ankles.

In the few seconds it took Jennie to retrieve the tool, Barlow managed to sit up. When Jennie approached, she lashed out with both feet. She missed Jennie, but knocked the pitchfork out of her hands.

Jennie retrieved it and held the tines within inches of Barlow's throat, forcing her to lie down again. "I meant it when I said I didn't want to hurt you, but I will if I have to. Turn over."

"You have no idea what you're getting yourself into."

Barlow's voice became more shrill with each word, but she did as Jennie said.

Jennie knelt beside Barlow, looped the wire around her ankles, inserted the handle through the loose coil and used it for leverage to wind the wire. She twisted until the stiff leather boots puckered and cinched inward.

"Ow!"

Jennie removed the handle and tugged on the wire. It was as tight as she could make it. She checked the knots in the scarf. Would they hold? Not forever. She didn't need forever—just enough time to get inside the barn and find the girls.

Chapter Thirty

The air inside the barn was stale, thick with hay dust, and smelled of disinfectant. After the brightness of the day, it seemed dark as midnight. Jennie tried to orient herself while she gave her eyes time to adjust. When she'd heard the girls, she'd been behind the barn; the sound had come from her left. *I'm facing the other way, so they're to my right.* The space was divided by an aisle running between two rows of stalls. On her left, the first stall was filled with bales of hay stacked high against one wall. Bags were lined up along another wall. Jennie called Jasmine's name.

"Here!"

She rushed toward the sound and found the girls in the back corner. Their legs were tied at the ankles, their wrists secured behind their backs. Jasmine sat next to a large support beam and was leaning against it. Fleur lay on her side.

"Thank God you found us." The tough-kid bravado

245

was missing from Jasmine's manner. At the moment, she seemed as much a child as Tommy or Andy.

Jennie knelt beside her and began to work on the knot binding her hands. "What happened?" she asked.

"Oooh!" There was a yelp of pain from Jasmine instead of an answer.

"Sorry." Jennie's eyes had adjusted to the dim light and she saw blood on the girl's wrists. "I have to pull the rope tighter to bring the end through the loop. It's going to hurt, but I'll try to make it quick." She kept her tone light and matter of fact, just as she did with her boys. She felt the tenseness in Jasmine's arms and back, but there were no more outcries. She worked as fast as she could and kept talking to distract her. "You get these sores trying to get loose?"

"Yeah. I tried to cut the rope by rubbing against that." Jasmine inclined her head toward the beam. "It works better in the movies."

"Still, it was good thinking."

"I had to do something. That nut was gonna kill us."

"Constance Barlow?"

"Yeah. Who'd a thought Miss Prissy Pants was dangerous?"

"Anybody can be dangerous if they're pushed into a corner." While she talked, Jennie pulled the end through the last loop. She patted Jasmine's shoulder. "Okay. Your hands are free. Think you can untie your legs while I take care of your sister?"

Jasmine brought her arms forward, then lifted them over her head in a stretching motion. She brought them back down and rubbed her thumb over the irritated flesh. She winced, but didn't cry out.

Jennie moved to Fleur and started working on the rope around her wrists. Fleur was rigid and hadn't said a word so far. Jennie leaned forward and looked into her eyes. "You okay, honey?"

Fleur still didn't speak, but she bobbed her head.

Jennie smiled at her. "Silly question," she said. "None of us will be okay until we get out of here. Right?"

Fleur smiled back. "Right."

"We're almost there." She freed Fleur's wrists and started on the rope binding her legs.

"Yes!" Jasmine removed the coil from her ankles and stood. She tottered and grabbed the beam to steady herself, but managed to remain upright.

"You're free too," Jennie said when she finished untying Fleur. She helped her to her feet. "Okay, both of you," she said, "walk around a little to get the circulation back."

Fleur did as she was told, but Jasmine protested. "I just want to get out of here."

"Look, we don't know what's waiting out there. We need to be ready to move fast if we have to. Just a few steps to get your sea legs."

The girls walked around the perimeter of the stall. "Swing your arms," Jasmine told Fleur. "And do this." She demonstrated by rotating her head and shoulders.

"I'm not sure I can. I'm too stiff."

Jasmine went to her sister and massaged her shoulders. "Better?" she asked.

"Yeah."

"Good. Now try this."

Fleur copied the motions her sister had demonstrated.

Jennie watched them in silence a few seconds. This was a side of Jasmine she'd never seen. Usually, Fleur was the mother figure, though she was two years younger. *Would my boys take care of each other like this. Oh, I hope so.* She shuddered at the thought of her sons being put to the test. "Let's get out of here," she said.

The girls followed Jennie down the aisle between the stalls. "How'd you get yourselves in this fix?"

"We were just—"

Jennie didn't hear the rest of what Jasmine said. They reached the door and went out into the sunshine. Constance was twisting her hands and had almost freed herself from the knotted scarf. Jennie called over her shoulder, "Go back and get some of that rope."

Jasmine scurried away without argument.

"What can I do?" Fleur asked.

Good question. Even better, what am I going to do?

Jasmine came back, trailing coils of rope.

Jennie picked up the pitchfork and handed it to Fleur. "I'm going to tie her up better. If she tries to get away, poke her."

Fleur looked back at Jennie with frightened eyes, but she accepted the tool.

"I'll do it," Jasmine said, and took the pitchfork from her sister. She held it close to Barlow's face. "Do something. I'd love to use this thing." She looked like she meant it.

Barlow drew her head back. "Don't I get to explain?"

Jennie removed the bloodstained scarf and used a piece of rope to retie Barlow's wrists. "That should hold." She spoke to herself as much as the girls. Then she looked at Constance. "Explain? Killing three people and kidnapping these girls? I'd love to hear what you have to say."

"I had to stop him."

Jennie said, "Atkinson?"

"Yes." The word came out like a missile.

"You admit you killed him?"

"What if it'd been your kids?"

"He gave steroids to your son?"

"Yes, and Bradley was never the same. The Barlow honor—"

"Honor?" Jennie couldn't believe she'd heard right.

"Our family's never had a suicide."

"Bradley's still alive."

"Fortunately, I found him in time. I just hope his new school can save him."

"Is the school in Florida a—"

"Never mind that. Forget my son. Leonard Atkinson had to be stopped."

"Why not go to the police? You made Mrs. Wyandotte sign a letter of recommendation. Instead of trying to stop him, you covered for him."

"I wanted him stopped permanently."

"But why Phillip Jeffries? What did he do?"

"That was an accident. I only meant for Leonard to get the poison." Constance faltered, almost seemed repentant. "It was dark in that hallway."

The pieces began to fall into place. Jennie said, "Between the kitchen and the dining room? Where servers put their orders on trays?"

Constance nodded and struggled to sit up.

One important piece was still missing. Jennie had to know. "What about Ann Tull? Did you do something to her car?"

She didn't answer, but it was clear from her face that she had.

"Why?"

"I wasn't going to spend the rest of my life in jail. Not for ridding the world of scum." There was no repentance in her tone now. "It was supposed to be you. I saw you watching me when I was on the balcony."

"You were on our balcony?" Jasmine shot a triumphant look toward Jennie.

"I'm sorry," Jennie said.

Jasmine ignored the apology and kept her eyes on Constance. "How'd you get up there?"

When Constance remained silent, Jennie said, "She's been touring your house for weeks, pretending she wants to buy it. She probably knows the layout better than you do." She looked toward Constance. "Right?"

"What about the poison?" Fleur asked.

Again, Jennie answered for Constance. "I guessing here, but I bet I'm close. She pretended to be talking to people in the dining room, listened to see what Atkinson ordered, then waited in the hallway outside the kitchen and slipped poison into his food when the server turned her back." She looked to Constance for confirmation.

Constance looked daggers back at her.

Jennie continued, "Then she slipped up the back staircase and—I'm guessing again—probably went through your mother's room out onto the balcony." She shuddered, remembering the horror of that night. "I still don't understand why."

"I told you. I wanted to do it myself." Constance was screaming now. She sounded more like a banshee than Martha had the night of the murder.

Jennie didn't buy it. "That's why we have laws. Police. Prisons."

"How long do you think he'd have stayed in prison?" Constance spit out the words.

"These girls? What'd you plan to do with them?"

"I wasn't going to kill them." Constance looked up at Jasmine, looming over her with the pitchfork, and at Fleur, standing nearby. "Really. I didn't want to hurt you."

Jasmine was no more convinced than Jennie was. "If you didn't want to hurt us, why'd you lure us out here?"

Jennie interrupted. "Wait a minute. She lured you out here?"

"Yeah," Jasmine said. "She called. We were supposed to meet this afternoon, but Mom wouldn't let us go. Said we had to do a family thing."

Fleur took over. "So Jas came up with the late movies story and we went last night."

"I just wanted to talk. I thought I could make you understand. I did it to help kids. Then when you called and said you were coming last night, I thought you were bringing the police. I couldn't let you come to my home. So I said to meet me in the lane near the old farmhouse." Constance had regained control. Her tone was sweetly reasonable, as if she still thought she might convince them to let her go.

Jennie ignored her and asked the girls, "Did you know she was the murderer?"

"Of course not. We're not dumb enough to meet a killer by ourselves."

Jennie was relieved to hear that.

"I didn't know what else to do." The words became sobs. The proud Constance Barlow had turned to jelly.

Jennie felt an uneasy sympathy, but she pushed it aside and turned to practical matters. "My phone's in the van on that road where you guys left your car. We're going to have to untie her legs, so we can walk back there. We'll call your mother and let her know you're okay. The police are there too. We'll let them take over and get you girls home." She looked at Jasmine. "To be safe, I want you to keep that weapon on her while I take the rope off."

"My pleasure."

Jennie knelt to untie the knot. As her fingers pulled the rope through the loop, she became aware of an ever-louder roar and looked up to see a white rectangle tearing across the field toward them.

Chapter Thirty-One

Can't be. Jennie looked again. *It is.*

A branch stuck in the front grill gave the impression someone had tried to camouflage it, but there was no doubt the charging rectangle was the vehicle used to transport the citizens of Riverview Manor. As it came closer, Georgie's head showed over the steering wheel—just. Her teeth were bared in an expression that was either sheer terror or unmitigated joy.

Jennie watched, spellbound as a mouse gazing into the eyes of a cobra. Whoa! She jumped aside as the van stopped amid a whirl of dust and hay—a scant six inches from where she'd been standing.

Georgie opened the van door and hopped out with a liveliness belying her ninety years. "I wasn't going to hit you," she said. "I was in total control at all times." Her grin, if possible, became wider.

The other ladies emerged from of the van, chattering

like twelve-year-olds at a sleepover. None were quite as nimble as Georgie, but this afternoon arthritis took a backseat to adventure.

Jennie did a quick head count. Everyone was there except Doreen. She looked up to see the missing tea lady tapping on a window. Jennie called to Jasmine. "Come help me with Doreen." She retrieved the keys from the ignition so she could unlock the back and get the wheelchair.

Jasmine passed the pitchfork off to Georgie and was in the van ahead of Jennie.

"Easy does it," Jennie positioned the chair, and Jasmine helped Doreen in. "All set?"

"Yes."

She started the van so the hydraulic lift would work.

As soon as she was safely on the ground, Doreen wheeled off to join the melee in front of the barn. She turned, almost as an afterthought, and sent a jaunty wave in Jennie's direction.

Jennie waved back, then looked around for her cell phone. She located it between the seats and started punching numbers.

Tess came over and leaned in the van door. She gestured toward Constance, who had raised herself to a sitting position, but whose hands and feet were still bound. "What happened?"

"Tell you later," Jennie said, without looking up. "Right now I have to make a phone call."

"Hello." Lilly answered on the first ring.

"The girls are safe."

There was a huge intake of breath, then a fainter

voice, as though Lilly had turned aside, said, "It's Jennie. She found your sisters. They're safe."

And a high, sweet voice, also faint, "Where are they?"

Lilly, speaking into the phone again, repeated the question.

Jennie said, "We're up here in River County. At the Barlow place."

"What're you doing there?"

"It's a long story. We'll explain when we see you."

"When will that be?"

"Soon, I hope."

"Can I talk to them?"

"Sure." Jennie gave herself a mental kick for not realizing that's what Lilly needed most right now. "Jas. Fleur. Your mother wants to talk to you."

Both girls dashed over. Jasmine grabbed the phone from Jennie. "Hey, Mom. We're okay." Then a pause and, "Really, we are. Yeah, both of us. Here she is." Jasmine handed the phone to Fleur.

Fleur took the phone and cradled it to her ear. "Hi. Yeah, honest." She nodded her head, listening. "We didn't mean to worry you. We thought we could help." Tears etched a jagged path through the dirt on her cheeks.

Jennie put her arm around Fleur's shoulder. "Can I have the phone now?" When Fleur handed it over, Jennie said to Lilly, "Sorry, but I have to make another call."

"But—"

"Look, I know you have a million things to say, questions and all, but there are other things I have to deal with, and the sooner I take care of them, the sooner I'll get your girls home."

There was a gutteral sound that could have been a sob, before Lilly said, "Go ahead, then, but hurry. Please, please hurry."

"I will, as much as I can."

"Just one more word with them?"

"Okay." Jennie handed the phone back to Fleur. "She wants to hear your voice again."

"Mom." The fourteen-year-old used the back of her free hand to wipe tears from her face. "I love you too." She stopped, took a deep breath. "Okay. Here's Jas."

Jasmine accepted the phone from her sister. "Mom, we're fine. Lot to tell you and Charly." A pause, then a mumbled, "Love you too," before she turned the phone over to Jennie. There was a suspicious brightness in the dark eyes, but no tears on Jasmine's cheeks.

Jennie punched in the number and tried to predict Goodley's reaction while she listened to the phone ring.

"Goodley here." Three perfectly enunciated syllables. No discernible emotion, not even impatience.

"Hi. It's me, Jennie."

"Where are you? Did you decide to take your ladies home?"

"Uh, not exactly."

"That means?" Now impatience reared its head, horns and all.

"We're at Constance Barlow's place. By the barn. Can you come right away?"

"Why?"

"I found the girls."

There was a sharp intake of breath.

"They're alive. Unharmed."

"Are you in danger?"

"No. Everything's under control." She hung up, not wanting to go into a lengthy explanation at the moment.

Her phone rang again. Immediately. She was tempted to let it ring, but decided against that. "What?"

"Under control? What does that mean?"

"We have the murderer. It's Constance Barlow, by the way. We're ready to turn her over to you." Then, because she couldn't resist, she added, "Isn't that the proper procedure?"

There was silence, then a hearty guffaw. "See you in a few minutes."

While Jennie had been on the phone, the ladies had encircled Constance and were bombarding her with questions. Georgie still held the pitchfork, obviously having the time of her life.

Jennie's memory flashed back to her first glimpse of Constance Barlow on the balcony that night, just a little over a week ago. She'd been so sure it was Jasmine, she hadn't looked further. If she had, would Ann Tull still be alive? Was Doreen wondering the same thing?

Jennie went to Doreen. "Have you heard the whole story yet?"

"What do you mean 'the whole story'?"

Jennie stopped, took a deep breath, and struggled to keep the tears welling in her eyes from falling. "You were right. She mistook Ann's car for mine." She gulped, spoke fast, determined to get the words out. "Because of that, Ann's dead."

Doreen took her hand. "Don't do this to yourself. It's not your fault Ann died. It's hers." She pointed to Constance, seated on the hay-strewn earth with her hands tied. "What you need to remember is how you saved these girls." She gestured toward Jasmine and Fleur, who couldn't seem to take their eyes off the pitchfork-wielding Georgie.

Jennie turned to survey the damage to the van. None of the windows were broken. That's good. She walked around the vehicle. Tires looked okay. Amazing. The paint job was a disaster. Scratches and dents all over. Her circuit complete, she stopped at the front and tried to pull the jagged piece of tree from the grill. It wouldn't budge. She pulled harder. A slight movement now. She pushed, thinking she could rock it, get some leverage and work it loose. Bad plan. The grill thudded to the ground and the tree lurched forward out of her hands. Now the windshield was cracked. *Leda's gonna have a cat!*

Chapter Thirty-Two

Jennie resisted the urge to lean on the horn when she pulled into the parking lot behind Lilly's. "Okay, girls, here you are. Safe and sound." The words didn't begin to convey all she was feeling. There probably were no words for that. She watched them bolt from the van and across the space to their back door. Fleur disappeared immediately. Jasmine turned at the last minute and looked at Jennie. "Aren't you coming up?"

"No. I'll talk to your mom later. You guys need some time."

Jasmine nodded, then disappeared after her sister.

Jennie turned to look at the ladies. "Your rooms are going to look pretty good to you about now."

No one argued with that.

Jennie noticed Ward's car in the lot as she backed out and headed across the alley and couldn't help but speculate how he fit into the picture.

* * *

It was a little after five when the scruffy-looking troup entered Riverview. The pre-mealtime bustle was in full swing so no one paid much attention to Jennie and the ladies.

Georgie staged a coughing spell that stopped traffic.

A teenage volunteer was the first to notice them. "Wow! What happened to you guys?"

The cough miraculously cleared up. "You can all stop worrying. The killer in our midst has been caught." Georgie paused to give her audience a chance to assemble, somehow managing to look both modest and all-powerful.

Doreen cut in before she could say more. "Why don't you let us freshen up? We'll be glad you to tell all about it after dinner. I, for one, am starving." Then she, Frances, Tess, Faye, and Vera all headed toward their respective rooms.

The onlookers drifted off toward the smell of roast chicken.

Georgie stood in the center of the hall with her mouth open, watching her audience ebb away. She shrugged philosophically and went to her room too.

Jennie had never felt so alone. She headed for the activities room, where she closed the door and made another phone call. *Maybe she won't be home.*

She was.

"Leda?"

"Jennifer? Is that you?"

"Yes."

"How'd your little outing go?"

"That's what I'm calling about. Things took an unexpected turn." She stopped for a breath, then plunged ahead. "The van is pretty much trashed."

"Trashed?" There was a long pause. "Is everyone okay?"

At least she asked the right question first. "Everyone's fine. It's just the van."

"Then you can tell me about it tomorrow. As for the van, we'll let the insurance company worry about it. I have to go now. I'm having a dinner party tonight. Possible contributors to Riverview. I know you don't think that's important, but if Riverview is going to continue to be the place we're so proud of, the money has to come from somewhere."

"Uh, Leda, you may want take time to watch the news before your guests arrive."

Another pause, this one longer. "You haven't done anything to reflect badly on Riverview?"

Had she? "I don't think so."

"That tone. I know that tone. Have you broken any laws?"

"No." Jennie made sure her tone was positive this time. "Actually, I think you may be proud of me and my ladies. Watch the news."

Jennie dialed Tom's number. Busy. *Well, he's expecting me. I'll just show up.* The leather jacket gaped open when she replaced the phone and she caught a glimpse of her reflection in the glass patio doors. Her hair looked like she was auditioning for a punk rock band. Blood stains covered the front of her shirt. *Kids can't see me like this. Better stop by the house and clean up.* The cell phone in her tote bag rang. She checked and wasn't surprised to see Goodley in the caller ID window.

"Hi."

"You okay?"

"Yeah, I got the girls and the ladies home and now I'm on my way to get cleaned up and go collect my kids."

"You feel like company tonight?"

"Uh, I just want to spend time with the kids."

"I could bring a pizza. No anchovies."

"That's sweet, but no. Thanks anyway."

"Okay, next week some time?"

She hated it when he was so nice. It was easier when he was mad at her. She hesitated, trying to find the right words.

He said, "I understand. Don't mean to be pushy."

"It's not that. I just, uh, I would like to get together sometime next week. We need to talk."

"I think I know what you want to say. I'll save you the trouble. You hope we can be friends. Right?"

"Yeah, something like that. But don't say friends like it's nothing. I take friendship seriously." The silence at the other end of the line was daunting. She continued anyway. "Wes, you're probably the nicest, most decent man I know. I appreciate that more than I've let you know."

She could hear his breathing, deep and even, over the phone and asked, "So, how about it? Can we be friends?"

"Nobody but a fool turns down an offer of friendship. So, how about a friendship dinner next week? You name the night."

"Wednesday?"

"Wednesday's good. Think you can stay out of trouble that long?"

"I'm sure gonna try."

She looked toward Lilly's when she got into her little Bug. Ward's car was still there. She glanced at her watch. Five twenty-five. She wondered what Lilly would do about Ward and Jasmine. Would she find the courage to stand up to her daughter? She wished she knew what the future held for Lilly and her girls. She shook her head. Impossible. Nobody ever knows that about anybody. She had a feeling things would never be the same. But "things" are never the same anyway.

Standing in the shower, she replayed her conversation with Wes and tried to analyze the mélange of relief and regret she felt. Had she done the right thing? *I really don't want a man in my life right now. Not even Tom?* That was the one question she couldn't answer. *Doesn't matter. He's involved with Maria and I have no right to interfere. I closed that door myself.*

She pulled the brightest red sweater she owned out of a drawer, threw on a pair of jeans and drove to Tom's, keeping at the upper edge of the speed limit. *Can't get a ticket. No time for that.*

She turned into the condo parking lot and looked toward Tom's balcony. Tommy and Andy must have been watching for her. They came out, waving madly, as she pulled into a parking space. She tapped the horn in salute. About them, at least, she was absolutely sure.